Now that at long last Warren had found Mercy, would her family intervene to keep them apart?

Warren's cold, bare hands cupped her cheeks. His thumbs gently caressed her temples, smoothing back her damp hair. Mercy's knees felt weak.

He sucked in a quick breath. "Mercy, I must say this quickly, before I lose courage. Your father refused to allow me to court you by letter; therefore, at long last, I am here to pursue my suit in person. I cannot tell you the suspense I suffered this past year, wondering if you had married another, praying that God would keep you healthy and free—for me."

Her eyes widened and her lips parted at his forthright declaration. She felt his hands become tense and knew by the look in his hooded eyes that he wanted to kiss her. Her hand lifted to rest upon his striped waistcoat.

The barn door suddenly flew open, letting in wind, rain, and two men.

JILL STENGL recently moved to Wisconsin where her family built a log home, glad to have years of moving with the military behind them. Jill considers herself a homebody and enjoys home schooling her four children, oil painting, quilting, sewing, and taking long walks with her husband and Fritz, a miniature schnauzer. She writes inspirational romance because that's what she most enjoys reading, and she believes that everything she does should be glorifying to God.

Books by Jill Stengl

Grant
Me Mercy

Jill Stengl

Heartsong Presents

With love to Michelle Smith and Paula Pruden-Macha, who freely offered their wise insights and advice—not to mention their constant encouragement. Only God can make women as wonderful as you two, my North Carolina friends. I see Jesus in your lives.

Thank you again to Teena Maultsby for giving me access to her extensive library on African-American history.

A note from the author:
I love to hear from my readers! You may correspond with me by writing: **Jill Stengl**
Author Relations
PO Box 719
Uhrichsville, OH 44683

ISBN 1-57748-966-7

GRANT ME MERCY

All Scripture has been taken from the King James Version of the Bible.

Cover illustration by Jill Stengl.

PRINTED IN THE U.S.A.

one

*But God, who is rich in mercy, for his great love wherewith he
loved us even when we were dead in sins, hath quickened us
together with Christ, (by grace ye are saved).*
Ephesians 2:4–5

Ontario, October 1813

He tried to open his eyes, but the effort was too great. He was aware only of pain, an icy numbing pain that intensified his longing to escape back into unconsciousness. *No, this cannot be!* his mind screamed in denial, yet the only sound that escaped his lips was a groan.

Something touched his face. He flinched and heard a voice speak as though from far away, "Eh, so you're not dead after all. Thought I heard somebody moan over here. Just you hold on, and we will have a litter this way soon as can be."

Then all was quiet, a deafening silence. Or was it only that his ears were forever damaged by the barrage of noise they had endured? Never would he escape the nightmare of that battle—his men had run like rabbits from the American cavalry charge.

Grinding his teeth against the pain, he became aware that his body was shivering. Here he would die in agony, and in a few months, his parents would receive notice of their son's fall on the battlefield. Lord willing, they would never know the exact circumstances of his death—shot down from behind while cursing in hopeless rage at his retreating troops.

God, are You there? Have mercy upon me, God. Nothing I have done in life has prepared me for a time such as this. I was not cowardly in battle, but I shall die as surely as did my craven companions. Will courage redeem me in Your sight? I think not.

Faces and scenes flashed through his mind—his parents, his brothers, his betrothed. Was this the end? He had heard that a man's life flashes before him when death approaches. He had no major sins in his past to confess—except for the major sin of disregarding God. *I thought it enough to be baptized and confirmed; now I know that such outward deeds are insufficient. My heart has never changed, and I know not how it can be changed. I am surely lost for eternity. God in heaven, help me! Grant me mercy.*

"Still breathing, are you?"

The gentle, drawling voice brought his eyelids fluttering open. "God?"

"No, but I am surely honored by your mistake." A pair of slate blue eyes peered down at him from beneath a fur cap. The man's voice was decidedly American.

"Mercy."

"I am here to help you, sir," the voice assured him. Another voice spoke in a questioning tone, and the first voice ordered, "Help me get this horse off him. Go easy. 'Tis a miracle he's alive. Can you imagine, after a night as cold as last night under pouring rain?"

"Poor fellow," a deep voice agreed.

Hands began working around his limbs. A weight lifted from his side, and agonizing pain ripped through him, dispelling his belief that his body had gone numb. He heard a scream from his own lips.

The first voice soothed, "You got yourself smashed up good, but I'll do my best to see that you make it. You keep right on talking to the Lord, sir. Sure as anything, He sent me to you; so you musta been praying right. Let's see, you're a captain?"

He could not shake his head, but his lips formed the answer no.

"Lieutenant?"

He mouthed "Yes." The orderly had mispronounced the title "Lewtenant," but that was the American way.

"Very well then, Lieutenant Redcoat, prepare for some rip-roaring pain in about two shakes."

Determined to endure, he clenched his teeth. Hands grasped his shoulders and ankles, and he was lifted upon a stretcher.

By the early morning light, he glimpsed his surroundings. The sight would haunt him to his grave. Bodies of men and horses lay scattered upon bloody, churned-up mud. Empty, staring eyes, limbs askew, spirits departed. Buckskin-clad Indians, British senior officers, and enlisted men, his friends and companions—all lay dead. And now, despite the admitted kindness of his captors, he was a prisoner of war.

He sank into oblivion.

&

Why, God? Why did You not allow us to defeat those arrogant backwoods Americans? Only partially conscious, the young British officer dreamed alternate prayers and curses.

The nerve of that nonentity General Harrison and his rag-tag cavalry to pursue and attack British forces on Canadian soil! This should never have happened; it is a travesty. This fraudulent, would-be nation of farmers and fishermen dares challenge England's authority on the high seas! True, our ships did impress a few American sailors and plunder an occasional ship back when America claimed neutrality—but France was far from innocent in that regard, and President Madison, that avowed Francophile, took no issue with her.

God, why did You not allow me to be assigned to the Continent with Wellington? There I might have been of genuine use in the all-important struggle against Bonaparte's tyranny. Here, I battle inept bunglers across the wilderness—

A voice interrupted his impassioned reverie. "Hold still and see if you can't swallow this, Lieutenant, sir. We've got to get more food into you if you're to see that gal of yours again."

The lieutenant's eyes fluttered open and tried to focus.

"What girl?" A spoon popped into his mouth, and he swallowed hard. Had someone laid a stone upon his chest? It was terribly heavy.

"The one you keep talking about. Haven't you got a girl named Mercy?"

"No."

Blue eyes crinkled. "My mistake. I got a sister we call Mercy, so I thought you were talking about a woman. Hey, Dunn," he raised his voice. "He's awake and talking. You were wrong, brother." He spooned another bite of broth into the lieutenant's mouth.

With a rush of wintry air, the tent flap opened and a large figure pushed inside. "Praise God!" A bearded face as dark as ebony appeared before the lieutenant's startled eyes and split into a wide smile. "Good to have you with us, sir. I am Private Dunn, and this joker is Private Jones."

The lieutenant decided he must have misunderstood. Surely this Jones fellow had not addressed the black man as "brother."

"Lieutenant Warren Somerville, 49th Rifles."

Private Jones of the slate blue eyes chuckled at his correct British pronunciation and shoved in another spoonful. "Pleased to meet you, Leftenant. Mind if I call you Lefty?"

The lack of deference for a foreign senior officer did not surprise him. These were, after all, Americans. With each spoonful of broth, the gnawing emptiness of his belly eased. "How long since the battle?"

"Three weeks tomorrow. You have talked to us before today, but I had a notion you weren't quite yourself. We had to transport you stacked like a log among other patients—that was no lark. Just as well you don't remember."

"My regiment?"

"Mostly dead. Some ran; others were captured. Our men burned Moraviantown. A shame, it was—not that your side hasn't fired more than one American town. You are in no condition to leave us for a while yet, but I'm sure you're important enough to rate an exchange when the time comes. We looked through your papers for identification."

"General Proctor?"

The roguish grin reappeared. "We nearly caught him, but he managed to slip away. That Indian chief Tecumseh was killed. It was quite a victory for our side. Never thought I'd see the day, since most of us went into this war with no experience whatsoever."

When Jones set the empty bowl on the floor, Somerville glanced around, seeing two other cots crowded into the small tent. Both were empty. "Is this a hospital?"

The two privates exchanged glances. "Of a sort," Jones muttered. "Here, eat this bread."

While the lieutenant obediently chewed, Private Dunn clarified the point. "Ever since you mistook my friend here for the Almighty, he took a personal interest in your recovery. After digging a chunk of smashed bone out of your shoulder, the doc wanted to remove your left leg at the hip. Jonesy wouldn't let him."

"These docs are known to get careless with a knife, and considering the location of your injury, I feared you might lose something more important than a leg." Jones grinned, but the smile faded as he looked into his patient's eyes. "Guess you don't think that's so funny. To be honest, the infirmary is crowded with American wounded, and the docs were disinclined to waste time or energy on a dying Brit. We wanted you to have a fighting chance, so we took you on as our private patient."

Somerville blinked, surprised by a feeling of gratitude toward his benefactors. "I thank you for your kind services. Am I expected to survive?" He brushed breadcrumbs from his empty hands. Although the food had helped, he still felt weak.

Dunn answered. "You took pneumonia, sir, but we believe you are through the worst of it. We didn't find you until the morning after the battle. Thankfully, you wore a greatcoat. Your horse might also have saved you, for you lay in the shelter of its body."

"Regis is dead." He remembered the gray stallion going down beneath him. There had been indescribable pain.

"Yes. He smashed your hip and leg when he fell against a downed log, but his body protected you from the cold. You also took a musket ball through your shoulder blade."

"Not to mention that your fancy cocked hat has a hole through its crown. God must have plans for your life, Lefty." Jones's cheerful voice held a serious note.

"I prayed to God for mercy."

"You certainly did. You have spoken of little else during your illness. So it is God's mercy you desire?" Jones inquired, his eyes lighting.

"All my life I have attended church, yet when I lay dying upon the battlefield, I knew not how to obtain God's mercy. Do you know how I can receive it?" His voice was weak, but his need was overwhelming.

The young man's face glowed. "Do we? Tell him, Dunn."

The young black man was already opening his Bible. "You came to the right place, Lefty; that's sure enough. No better place to learn about God than from His Book. I shall begin reading with Paul's letter to the Ephesians, starting—"

"You can read?"

Dunn's smile faded slightly. "I took schooling along with the young master back home in Maryland. His father, the old master, made certain all the house servants learned to read and cipher."

"You have the speech of an educated man, I had observed. Are you his slave?" He glanced toward Jones.

"No, sir. I came to war in place of my master's son. After the war ends, I shall have my freedom." Private Dunn spoke quietly.

"A difficult means to earn it."

"Yes, sir, but freedom is well worth the price. I met Jonesy when I joined the army, and he taught me about Jesus, who loves all men equally no matter what color their skin. Now I am free on the inside, where it counts most. Even if I die before this war ends, I've got my freedom."

"Amen, brother." Jones squeezed his companion's wide shoulders, then gave him an affectionate punch on the arm.

Somerville had never before seen a white man embrace a black man. Never. There was something unique about these two, something fine and good. "Yes, read to me from the Book, please. Tell me how my spirit can be free."

It was all the invitation Dunn needed. The black soldier read in his rich voice: "Blessed be the God and Father of our Lord Jesus Christ, who hath blessed us with all spiritual blessings. . . . In whom we have redemption through his blood, the forgiveness of sins, according to the riches of his grace. . . . The eyes of your understanding being enlightened; that ye may know what is the hope of his calling. . . . For by grace are ye saved through faith; and that not of yourselves: it is the gift of God: not of works, lest any man should boast."

For nearly an hour, Private Dunn read passages from the New Testament. When he paused, his patient requested more.

Lieutenant Warren Somerville's eyes of understanding were enlightened that day, and after twenty-one years of aimless wandering through life, he at last understood the hope of God's calling. While Dunn and Jones knelt beside his cot, he prayed a formal little prayer straight from his heart, obtained mercy, and entered into the family of God.

two

Be kindly affectioned one to another with brotherly love;
in honour preferring one another.
Romans 12:10

A few evenings later, Somerville sipped a steaming cup of sumac tea and watched Private Jones read a letter by candlelight. "Communication from home?"

Jones's lean face was gray with fatigue. He had worked a double shift in the infirmary that day, then returned to his tent to care for Somerville. "First mail we've had in weeks. Guess it will be a while before you hear from home, eh? Are you warm enough? I'll tuck Dunn's blanket around your feet here. He won't mind; he is on duty. It's just you and me until midnight. We need to keep him in prayer; it's deadly cold out there."

"Are you certain your superior officers know that I am in your tent? Will you not suffer discipline for your kindness to me?" The laxity of discipline in this encampment amazed Somerville. Brushy beards and long hair, scruffy uniforms mixed with buckskin and furs—this army was unlike any in his previous experience.

Sometimes at night he heard swearing and revelry from surrounding tents, the screaming laughter of female camp followers, the drunken shouts of lonely, bored soldiers; but inside this small tent, all was peaceful and good. A few other soldiers occasionally gathered within to listen while Jones or Dunn read Scripture; some men refused to enter a black man's tent under any circumstances.

"Colonel Gordon doesn't care if you're here as long as we attend our American patients properly. You're the only Redcoat we've got left alive that hasn't been exchanged or imprisoned. Soon as you're up and around, you'll be shifted to the stockade. I'd take my time recovering, if I was you."

"How is it that you share a tent with Dunn?" Warren had been wondering for days.

"He got stuck in our group. Must have been a slip-up. He's the only black man for miles, and no one would even speak to him. My Quaker mother taught me that God looks at a man's heart, not at the color of his skin, so who was I to judge the man unworthy of my friendship? Now he is my brother in the Lord and the best friend I ever had. The army may have slipped up, but God planned it all the time." Jones's crooked teeth showed in his charming grin.

Warren blinked. He had never thought of it that way.

"Are you from Kentucky?"

"Nope. I volunteered to serve where I was needed. They gave me some medical training and threw me in with this rowdy Kentucky crowd. I hail from North Carolina."

"You were not among the ranks of our attackers?"

"Nope," Jones said again. "Dunn and I are on the clean-up crew."

Although fighting was not his idea of a pleasant task, Warren thought it vastly preferable to the job of picking up casualties on the battlefield, holding down a screaming man while a doctor sawed off a shattered limb, or burying countless unnamed corpses. No wonder Dunn and Jones often looked exhausted and drained of life.

"Finish your tea? Nasty stuff, ain't it? My granny swears by it as a tonic for whatever ails you. Her mother's mother was Cherokee, and she passed on all kinds of native medicine lore. Want me to read more Scripture tonight? We're in First Timothy now. Good information about a Christian's walk with God. Now that you're His child, you need to know how He wants you to live in this world."

"Yes, but first tell me, how is your sister Mercy?"

Jones grinned. "Fine and dandy. She always mails a letter along with the one from my parents. She knows I'll pay the

postage because her letters are the best." He gave Somerville
a second look. "Want to hear?"

"If you do not object."

"Stop me when you get tired. She begins: 'Dear Calvin.'
That's me, by the way."

Somerville nodded encouragingly.

The young Southerner tugged a raccoon cap down over his
ears. Sandy hair straggled from beneath it. "Cold is getting to
me. Sure you're warm enough?"

"I am comfortable. Please read on." The odor from his
bearskin coverlet annoyed him at times, but it was wonder-
fully warm. It was strange, how free and relaxed he felt—a
prisoner lying on a rough cot inside an American encampment. Just as Dunn had said, his freedom was on the inside
where it mattered most.

He smiled, lay back, and closed his eyes, letting Calvin
Jones's Southern drawl flow over him.

Dear Calvin,

*I just put Knox and George down for their naps. At
last, they sleep! I feared George would never stop crying.
You would scarcely recognize our baby brothers, for they
are growing quickly. Knox calls me "Bursy" and wants
me to sing and rock him before he will sleep. Granny
says I have spoiled the two past recall, but everyone is
pleased when I make them stop screaming.*

*We have received no word from Cliff, and Ma worries
about him. I think he has gone to Kentucky. It is hard for
Pa to lose his help at the forge.*

"Cliff is seventeen, the second son," Calvin explained in an
aside. "He always did have a wanderlust. I don't know how Pa
will manage the smithy without him. Poor little Will doesn't
have the strength for the job; he is only eleven and a skinny
kid. I hope Pa doesn't lose his business since Cliff left. I don't
know what he would do."

"How old are your other sisters and brothers?"

"Mercy is fourteen, Julianne is, uh, nine, and Helen is. . .I think she's five, and, well, Knox and George are mostly babes yet. Ma lost a few younguns in between."

"Your brother's name is Knocks?"

"Knox, as in John Knox Jones. All us boys are called after famous preachers, like our pa; he's Martin Luther Jones. I'm John Calvin Jones, then there's John Wycliffe Jones, William Penn Jones, and George Fox Jones."

Somerville looked dazed. "Read on."

Calvin returned to the letter.

Pa needs an apprentice, but there are few young men left in town. How I wish I were a boy!

Julianne is still sickly, always wheezing. Granny ladles that nasty tonic into her and makes her drink sumac tea every morning. I feel so sorry for my poor sister! I often see Pa gaze at her with worry in his eyes; you know how he dotes upon our angel-girl. Helen is sturdy like me, thank the Lord, and she works hard at her chores.

I raced Lemuel Griffith after school yesterday and beat him. Afterward he tried to throw me, but I knocked him down. Pa whipped me when I came home with my nose bloodied, but I cannot see that this was fair, for I did not start the fight. Granny says I am becoming a hoyden and that I should try to behave like a lady. What is a hoyden, Calvin? Do you think I am becoming one? I dislike boys when they try to show me how strong and superior they are, that is all.

Mr. Hezekiah is no longer allowed to teach mixed classes of black children and white children. Some parents complained. Now the black children must take their lessons at night after we go home. I do not see the sense in this, for are we not all children? Mr. Hezekiah is black himself, after all, and he is the best schoolmaster I have ever had. Granny still insists that I should stay home and not fill my head with useless book learning, but Mama prevails.

Tell me what you are doing, Calvin. I long to hear about the world outside this town. Do you often see British soldiers and Indians? I know that you assist doctors, but do you ever have to fight? I hope not. I try not to worry, but sometimes I miss you terribly and cannot help but cry. There is no one here who talks with me the way you do. Please hurry and win the war so I can have you back to be my big brother.

I love you and send many hugs and kisses.

"And so on and so forth," Calvin ended.

Somerville was silent. No doubt believing the officer asleep, Calvin quietly folded the closely written page and placed it inside his Bible.

He was far from sleep. "Does she resemble you?"

"In some ways. Her eyes are the same color. Got long arms and legs like mine—skinny as a beanpole. However, she is quick on her feet, strong as an ox, and mighty smart. She would have made a doughty man, no doubt, but I like her fine as a girl. The world needs more like her. We could use a dose of Mercy medicine around these parts."

Somerville's lips softened. "What color is her hair?"

"Kind of brownish. Julianne has hair like gold and skin like pearl, but poor Mercy got freckles. She might turn out well, though the trend isn't promising." Cal grinned. "She's just fourteen, so there is hope yet."

"Her given name is Mercy?"

"Mercedes, but I always call her Mercy. Ma doesn't like it; she goes for the high-falutin' names. Pa chose us boys' names, but Ma gets to name the girls. She comes from fine Quaker stock—she is distantly related to Mrs. Madison, the president's wife, and is she proud of it. I should say! Anyway, Pa tends to favor Julianne because she's pretty like Ma, and frail. Not even Granny dares order Julianne around much. Not that I don't love Julianne—she's an angel—but so is Mercy, in a different way." He paused. "Sorry. Didn't intend to bore you."

"You do not bore me; on the contrary. Will you write back to Mercy?"

"Sure will. I'll tell them about you. Want me to put in a word from you for Mercy?"

Somerville opened his eyes. "Were I to write her, would she receive the letter?"

"Picking up mail at the store is Mercy's job, but Ma might frown on her receiving letters from a man. Why the sudden interest in my sister?"

He pondered the question. "Perhaps it is her name. I begged God for mercy, and He is most generous." A smile glimmered in his deep eyes.

"Don't you have a woman in England? You did mention a lady once." Calvin lifted one brow. "Is she so quickly forgotten?"

"Mellisande. She can hardly be jealous of a child." The eyes darkened, returning to their usual somber expression. "I have received no letters from her since my regiment sailed."

"Perhaps her letters were lost."

"It is possible. Actually, I did not expect her to write. We are. . ." Uncertain how to explain their relationship, he fell silent.

"Let me guess—one of you is rich and the other carries a title."

"I possess no title; though the Somerville name is well known. I am my father's third son and receive only a modest annuity from my mother's estate. With my best welfare in mind, my parents purchased a commission for me and arranged this match with their neighbor's only child, who stands to inherit a sizable property. I have known Mellisande since she was a babe in leading strings."

"Is she pretty?"

"Very pretty."

"Now don't you sound the passionate lover," Calvin

chuckled. "You've got no more expression than a stick of wood. Maybe you do need a firebrand like my little sister to warm your chilly English blood."

An acknowledging smile glimmered in Somerville's eyes. "Tell me more about her. Does she trust in Jesus?"

"Yes. She prayed with me a few years back and gave her heart to the Lord. That was after—well, it's a long story. Sure you want to hear me rattle on like this?"

"Positive. Rattle on."

Needing little encouragement, his roommate blew out the candle, lay back on his cot, and talked himself to sleep. Long after the drawling voice ceased, Somerville stared into the darkness, trying to picture a gangling girl with slate blue eyes.

⁂

It was Christmas Eve, and the temperature had once again dropped below zero. Icicles adorned tent flaps, and trees crackled beneath an icy glaze. Fingers and toes remained cold at all times, no matter how many gloves or socks the soldiers wore. There had been talk of shifting camp, but no one expected to move until this cold snap ended. Many soldiers took refuge in the bars and public houses of a nearby town during their off-duty hours.

Somerville had recently been moved to the log stockade. Due to his inability to walk without a crutch and assistance— also due to his rank—he had been assigned a private room with some amenities. Prison, however, was prison.

A pair of dirty white breeches hugged his legs, straining over his bandaged left hip and thigh; his proud red coat was very much the worse for wear. He had no changes of clothing; his knapsack had not been recovered from the battlefield. Looters had probably stolen it before the medics arrived on the scene. For the duration of his captivity, he would have to make do with a bloodstained, torn uniform. His oilskin great-coat had disappeared during his sojourn in the infirmary. Only his boots still gleamed as a British officer's should, thanks to Oscar Dunn.

The wound in his right shoulder had healed over, leaving matched red scars on his back and chest. His hip and leg gave him considerable discomfort and probably always would. Determined to regain as much mobility as possible, he endured the pain with stiff-upper-lip doggedness.

Incapacity was a grievous affliction for a man of his independent nature; lack of fresh clothing was a sore trial for a man of his fastidious habits. If not for daily visits from Jones and Dunn, he might have fallen into despair.

Rumor suggested he would soon be exchanged for a high-ranking American officer. Although he would be thankful to see the last of this vile stockade with its smells and privations, he was by no means certain he wanted to return to England. No longer would he live comfortably within the confines of its rigidly stratified society. He felt closer to Jones and Dunn after a few weeks in their company than he had felt to his British mates after years of association. The Lord made the difference, he was well aware. Even a few months earlier, he, a Somerville of Colvert Hall, would have scorned association with poor white trash like Jones—and friendship with a black man? Preposterous. Utterly absurd.

Yet now these two odd Americans were like brothers to him. Leaving them would be like leaving family—in some ways worse, for they would again become his enemies. Not that he would fight any future battles. His warring days were over. He wanted to settle down, raise a family, and serve God in this brave young country.

Such disloyal aspirations could be dangerous.

"Prisoner," a voice called from outside the warped door. "You have visitors."

"Let them enter, please." He pushed himself up to a sitting position on the cot.

The guard stuck his head through the doorway for a moment. "Ten minutes, Lieutenant. That's all. Sorry."

"Understood."

Calvin entered in a rush, bringing icy outside air with him.

"Merry Christmas, Lefty!" Oscar Dunn followed, giving his peaceful smile.

"Now that you are here, it is indeed." Warren's heart warmed at sight of his friends.

"And we bring Christmas cheer. Look at this! Socks and a muffler, and a box of dried fruit: plums, peaches, grapes, and figs. Nuts, too." Unrolling a bundle, Calvin tossed two woolly blobs at the Englishman. "We each got some; they're from my family. My mother and Mercy knitted those."

Warren gathered thick brown socks and a scarf into his hands, staring in disbelief.

"Wait till you try this fruit. It's like a taste of summer." Calvin set a box on the foot of Warren's cot. "Not only that, but Mercy wrote letters, and Will, my artist brother, sent drawings."

The British officer swung his legs over the side of the cot. His left leg was stiff, but he had limited use of it. He struggled to pull a new sock over the one already on his foot. "Mercy wrote to me?"

"Christmas cheer, she explains in my letter. She couldn't bear the thought of you and Oscar passing Christmas with no word from family and friends, so she sent you each a letter and a gift. God must have known how greatly we all needed an encouraging word right about now. Dunn and I already read our letters. You can read yours later—but I think you might enjoy seeing these pictures now." He tossed two folded papers into Somerville's lap. "Not bad likenesses. William Penn Jones has a future as a cartoonist, I would say."

Somerville picked up the drawings. Each member of the Jones family had been depicted in pencil; they were amateur sketches, yet remarkably accurate in detail. Here, a girl bent over two small boys and scrubbed their pouting faces. It was Mercy, he knew. A long braid dangled over her slim shoulder, and her face showed tender care for her baby brothers.

Here, an old woman pinned a child's pinafore. There was a sketch of a man shoeing a horse, and another of a woman milking a sour-faced goat. Another showed two young girls reading, the older child's hair in curls over her shoulders. *Julianne the angelic,* he supposed.

Somerville's favorite sketch was the most lifelike. Mercy sat with her back against a tree, gazing into space. Her young brother must have caught her daydreaming and had used his artistic opportunity well. Deft pencil strokes had caught the tilt of her head, the curves of her cheek and throat.

"Your brother is eleven?"

"No, come to think of it, he's twelve now. I lose track."

"Indeed, he is gifted. These are remarkable, particularly in view of his age. May I have this one? I would cut it off carefully."

"If you want that drawing, it's yours. It looks a lot like her. Seems like you cherish a *tendre* for my little sister." Calvin sounded amused yet sympathetic.

"I did not realize that French was spoken in North Carolina." The lieutenant frowned at Calvin's teasing. Borrowing Dunn's knife, he sliced the coveted drawing from the page, then placed it and the letter inside his waistcoat.

Calvin chuckled. "We've heard plenty of French these past months, in and out of Canada. Say, our time is short. Would you like Dunn to read the Christmas story before we go?"

"I would greatly appreciate it." Warren's pale face brightened.

Bending closer to the flickering candle beside Warren's bed, Oscar Dunn quickly opened the Bible to the second chapter of Luke and read aloud. Tears stood in Warren's eyes when the ageless story ended. "Jones, Dunn, I have no words to express my appreciation for your friendship." He waved a hand over his rich gifts.

Calvin wrapped a friendly arm around the British officer's shoulders. "You're family, Lefty, our brother in Jesus Christ. It's a bond that will last for eternity."

"Amen." Oscar took Warren's offered hand in his huge brown grasp.

Gray eyes met brown, and Warren returned the black man's

smile. "For eternity," he echoed.

"Let us ask for God's blessing," Oscar suggested gruffly. The three men bowed their heads, and each spoke a short prayer, thanking God for each other, praising Him for His faithfulness, and requesting guidance and wisdom for the future.

The guard poked his head through the doorway again. "Time's up."

Calvin and Oscar stepped back, blinking and clearing their throats. "Yup. We're just leaving," Calvin said. The guard disappeared again.

Turning back to Warren, Calvin waved airily. *"Adieu, mon ami.* Or, as you Brits prefer, go with God, my friend."

"I understand French, Private Jones." Warren growled.

"You, *mon ami grincheaux,* could find use for a sense of humor."

"I am not your grouchy friend," Somerville protested in feigned irritation, "and your pronunciation is execrable."

Jones and Dunn chuckled.

The lieutenant's expression softened, and one corner of his mouth lifted. "You two would find sources of amusement at your own funerals, I have little doubt. Have you finished baiting the bear? Go on with you now." His voice held a wealth of affection.

His visitors took their leave, promising to return upon the morrow. "I'll bring my letters, in case you want to read them," Calvin promised.

The tiny room seemed colder after their departure. Warren sighed and leaned his head back against the rough log wall. Cold seeped through the chinking. He shivered and wrapped his bearskin—Calvin's "spare"—around his shoulders.

He picked up the precious letter bearing his name in rounded, girlish script. Smiling faintly, he broke the seal and unfolded it.

Dear Lt. Somerville,
I trust that you will not think me overbold in writing to

a man whom I have never met. Calvin wrote about you, about your terrible injuries, your recent salvation and commitment to the Lord, and your decision to become a minister upon your return to England. He also reports that he has read my letters to you and told stories about me. I hope that he has related only favorable tales, though I sadly fear otherwise.

Is it true that you begged God for mercy while you lay dying upon the battlefield? The story caused me to shudder and thrill by turns as I pictured your harrowing plight and God's miraculous intervention in sending my brother to your aid. How thankful I am that Calvin was able to aid you, sir! Often I have prayed earnestly for his rapid return, but now I see that you needed him there far more than I needed him here. I am thankful that God answered me No and you Yes.

I almost feel as though I know you, and I wish to do all that lies within my power to bring Christmas joy to your heart. You must miss your family and friends terribly; I hope they know of your survival. Rest assured that far away in North Carolina, one person will be thinking of you and praying for you each day, and especially on Christmas Day.

As I lie here in the loft beside my sisters, writing by the light of a candle, I can almost picture you, Calvin, and Private Dunn reading the Bible and praying together. Calvin says that you and Private Dunn sing like an angel duet. I wish I could hear you. I am thankful that my brother has fellowship with two wonderful godly men. If ever this war ends, I hope that Calvin will invite his friends here to meet his family. You and Private Dunn would be most welcome in our midst, but take note—I shall insist that you sing for us!

I must finish, for my quill needs trimming and my candle has nearly guttered. This is my penalty for saving your letter till last! You will no doubt think me bold, but I

feel that you are in need of loving compassion. Therefore
I send herein a warm embrace and kiss your cheek as a
little sister in Jesus. May the joy and promise of
Christmas warm your lonely heart this day.

With kindly affection from your
Mercy Jones

Three times he read the letter, lingering over special phrases. A glorious fire seared his inward parts as he pored over her written hug and kiss. Never in his life had anyone spoken or written to him such open declarations of admiration, sympathy, and affection. In his family, affection had been presumed, never verbally expressed or outwardly demonstrated. People had often called him cold and indifferent, which was grossly untrue. His emotions were as real and powerful as those of any man; he simply kept them under careful control. It was the Somerville way.

She calls herself my Mercy, Lord.

Not even to God could he express the yearning in his heart, a longing for tender, compassionate love such as Mercy's artless letter had offered. Here in the dank, comfortless stockade he could imagine the touch of a girlish hand upon his shoulder, soft lips against his cheek, and a loving hug. The fact that Calvin had described the girl as freckled, lanky, and shapeless had no effect upon Warren Somerville's lonely dreams. Mercedes Jones was soft and warm where it mattered most: in her heart.

That night Warren composed a letter, struggling to keep his ink from freezing before he put it to paper.

Dear Miss Jones,

At this point he squeezed his eyes shut and fought back a wave of emotion. This battle with sentiment was new to him. When the Lord entered his heart and filled it with love, had He smashed all of Warren's longstanding emotional barriers and safeguards? At times it seemed so. Recently he found it incredibly, distressingly easy to smile, laugh, or even cry.

You can have no conception of the joy your gifts and letters brought to me this Christmas Eve. Instead of resembling every other day in its boredom and routine, this day is filled with joy and thanksgiving. My feet are warm, my neck is comfortable, and my mouth is filled with sweetness. Best of all, I have your gift of words to read and read again.

I no longer reside with your brother and Oscar; I have been transferred to the stockade. However, my faithful friends visit me daily, no matter the weather. Should you write me again, Calvin can deliver your letter. I humbly solicit continued correspondence with you.

I thank you for your kindness to me, my little friend, and I thank you in particular for the benevolence that prompted your gifts. Yours is the only embrace and yours the only kiss I will receive this Christmas—but at present they suffice to fulfill my heart's every longing. When I implored God's mercy, I could never have imagined the extent of mercy He would bestow. You signed your letter "Your Mercy" and so you are mine forevermore.

If I live through this conflict and if God so pleases, I shall visit the Jones homestead in North Carolina as you and Calvin both have requested. Perhaps Private Dunn and I will sing for you someday—only our Lord knows the future.

As often as you read this letter, be reminded that I am your devoted servant,

Warren Johnstone Somerville

three

Hope deferred maketh the heart sick,
but when the desire cometh, it is a tree of life.
Proverbs 13:12

North Carolina, October 1819

Mercy Jones lifted her head as the parson said, "Amen." Her tingling spine prompted a quick glance around her poke bonnet's curved brim. Sure enough, the visitor was looking at her again. First Church's carved walnut pews had low backs and hard seats to prevent worshipers from falling asleep, but they could not prohibit wandering minds and eyes. Although Mercy had attempted to concentrate and take notes on the minister's sermon, she was well aware that a handsome man had cast his gaze across the aisle many times that day.

She could not imagine why this stranger would give her a second look, let alone his almost undivided attention. It made her nervous, albeit, deep inside, it also gave her a thrill. Or was he actually looking at Letty, seated beside her? In her new pale green bonnet and apricot dimity dress, Letty Wentworth did look pretty today.

When the congregation began to disperse, Mercy saw the distinguished stranger enter the center aisle. She kept track of him by sneaking peeks in his general direction, pretending to search for someone else. He paused at the end of the Wentworth pew, then strode on toward the foyer, limping slightly. Mercy tucked her pencil and notes into her reticule and pulled its strings tight.

"Do you know that man, Mercy?" Letty asked as soon as he had disappeared through the door. "Mother says he arrived in town yesterday and is staying at the tavern. He has not yet come into our store, or I would surely have taken note. Is he not fine?"

"I did not observe him," Mercedes Jones said, retying her bonnet strings. She glanced up at the ceiling and winced as though lightning had struck in answer to her outright lie. "Thank you for asking me to sit with your family this morning."

" 'Twas my pleasure, darlin'. I could hardly leave you to sit alone. I cannot recall the last time your family was not in church. Are they all ill?"

"The boys are nearly recovered from the ague and longing to get out and about, but Granny, Helen, and Julianne awakened quite ill this morning. Papa said he would manage without me today because Granny desired me to take sermon notes for her. I suppose I'll come down with the sickness next."

"You? You haven't been ill since we all took the measles three years ago."

A pained expression crossed Mercy's face, and Letty suddenly remembered. "Oh, I'm sorry. I didn't mean to remind you—"

"I know. It is only that I miss them so. Granny tries to care for us, but she. . .well, she is not Mama. And William. . .if Oscar hadn't come to help Papa in the forge, we would be in terrible straits by now with no sons old enough to assist him."

"The Lord did provide for your family by sending that black man, didn't He? Papa doesn't approve of paying wages to freed slaves; he says it gives proper servants wrong ideas. But I suppose your father was desperate. Yes, I do recall that Oscar was your brother's war friend; you needn't remind me. Anyway, let us speak of happy things—like handsome men!"

Entirely willing to avoid discord, Mercy smiled. "Yes, let's do."

The two girls followed Letty's parents down the aisle. Letty smoothed her skirt and practiced batting her big green eyes. "How do I look?"

Mercy pursed her lips, eyeing her friend's frock. "You look

lovely, Letty, as you well know. That color brings out the roses in your cheeks." In the foyer, the girls shook the vicar's hand, then claimed their wraps. Mercy pulled her knitted shawl close around her shoulders, feeling dowdy beside her companion. Although her own linsey-woolsey dress was undoubtedly warmer than Letty's frock, at the moment, Mercy would have sacrificed practicality for beauty.

"If only he would notice me," Letty sighed in her dramatic way, casting woeful glances toward the gentleman across the churchyard. As the girls descended the stone steps, Letty lifted the collar of her silk-lined cloak and shivered in the autumn breeze. She was not generally considered a beauty, for her front teeth protruded noticeably, but her fine clothes and figure almost compensated for this minor defect. Since Mr. and Mrs. Wentworth owned the village general store, their daughter always modeled the latest styles in hats and gowns.

"But Letty, what of Howard Steele? I thought you were deeply in love with him."

"Oh, Howard." Letty sounded startled by the thought. "Yes, I do adore Howard, but he is away in Charleston this month." She stood on tiptoe and craned her neck to keep the visitor in sight. "Do you see him, Mercy? You are taller than I."

"Letty, you fickle creature, do not make a scene! We are blocking the steps standing here. Oh dear, it rained again during church. I hope it does not begin again until I am home." While she talked, Mercy took her friend by the arm and headed up a slope on the far side of the churchyard. There, from the partial shelter of a large chestnut tree, the girls examined the object of their interest while he conversed with another parishioner.

"Is he not comely? Such brooding eyes, and that exquisite nose! Papa says he must have been in the military: he stands so straight. Have you noticed that he limps? Just enough to be interesting. He has very fine legs and shoulders, though he is perhaps a bit thin. Howard has broader shoulders, but then his legs are too heavy."

"Letty, the way you talk!" Mercy gasped, although she had already noticed the visitor's athletic physique. He had the look of a man who spent many hours in the saddle—muscular legs and trim torso—emphasized by his polished Hessian boots and sweeping overcoat.

"I hope he has no dreadful scars." Letty mused. "Look! He searches for someone, glancing around while Mr. Edmonds drones on and on at him. Perhaps he is seeking me!"

Or me. But then Mercy's practical side pushed to the forefront. "He is probably quite wild, addicted to racing and cards, and wholly unsuitable for a proper young lady to know."

"Isn't every handsome young man of fortune? I am simply dying to meet him. Mother says he is English, and I love an English accent. He has a noble-sounding name, although I cannot recall it to save my life. I will wait counters this week, for he surely must come to the store sometime."

As soon as Mr. Edmonds stopped talking, another man claimed the visitor's notice. Mercy watched him nod politely and return the greeting; although, as Letty had observed, he seemed impatient to move on.

"You say he is English?" Mercy's heart leaped. Could it be? *Lieutenant Somerville promised he would come.* The man did fit Calvin's description of his dapper British friend. But after long months of silence, Mercy dared not allow her hopes to soar.

"Ooh, Papa is speaking to him! I wonder if he will invite him to visit us." Letty grabbed Mercy's arm and hopped up and down in a most undignified manner. "I must ask Mother. I shall see you later, Mercy." She hurried down the slope toward her parents, unable to restrain a little skip of excitement every few steps. In many ways, Letty seemed younger than her nineteen years.

Mercy was grateful that she had not voiced her thoughts. It was highly unlikely that this gentleman had any connection with Lieutenant Somerville. Besides, Letty had always derided

Mercy's long-distance romance. Of all things, Mercy dreaded mockery. She had endured enough of it to last a lifetime.

Mercy tried to be excited and hopeful on her friend's behalf but found it difficult. As a successful merchant, Letty's father moved freely among the higher echelons of local society. Mercy's father, a struggling blacksmith in the same village, was a virtual nobody. The discrepancy was difficult for Mercy to accept at times. Nevertheless, Letty was a good friend.

Not good enough, however, to think of offering Mercy a ride in the Wentworth carriage. Letty did tend to be selfish where men were concerned. Chewing on her lower lip, Mercy watched the visitor speak with the Wentworths. Letty curtsied her prettiest and offered her small hand. The gentleman took it and bowed rather stiffly.

"Dear God," Mercy sighed, "Forgive my envy of Letty. She cannot help being lovely and rich. How I wish a fine gentleman would desire to meet me!" After one last longing look, she turned and began to weave her way between headstones toward the back of the graveyard. Rather than trek down the muddy road, she would take a short cut across Hiram Doore's property. Soggy autumn leaves lay thick upon the ground and felt mushy beneath her feet. Although Mercy wore heavy boots instead of slippers, she chose her footing with care.

She paused on top of the stile in the graveyard wall and looked out over the countryside. First Church was set on a low hill a short distance from town, one of few relatively high spots along the coastal plain. Mr. Doore's grandfather had donated the rather inconveniently located site. From her perch atop the stile, Mercy viewed mile after mile of tangled wilderness. Cultivated fields and a few clusters of buildings dotted the expanse, but much of North Carolina remained untouched by man's refining influence. Thick gray clouds occluded the sky, looking especially threatening toward the west.

Clasping both hands behind her head, Mercy stretched luxuriously while wind gusts rippled her skirts around her legs. Her faded brown dress allowed freedom of movement, though it did little to highlight her lithe figure.

"I should have outgrown romantic fancies by my age," she rebuked herself, speaking with the acquired wisdom of twenty years. "I shall probably remain a spinster until age forty, then marry a fat, bald widower who wants me only to raise his unruly brood, since I have abundant experience caring for children."

Thus tossing aside her dream, she jumped off the stile and started running downhill at an angle to meet the road farther down. Her straw bonnet fell to her shoulders. Twigs grasped at her coiled braid, tweaking it into an untidy tangle. Her shawl caught on a prickly bush; she pulled it loose and trotted on, slowing to a jog as the ground leveled out. Just ahead lay the fence that divided Hiram Doore's property from the church road.

Panting and rosy, Mercy felt invigorated. It was pure joy to exercise her strong body and fill her lungs with fresh air. For a few blessed moments she could forget about a crowded cabin filled with feverish, whining little bodies and endless chores.

A carriage rattled and bumped along the rutted road, spewing mud in its wake. Mercy ducked back into the brush and waited until it had passed before peeking out. It was the minister's old buggy. He was usually last to leave the church. The other parishioners had already passed this point in the road, heading either toward their plantations or into town.

Circles rippled across the standing water in the road's deep ruts; a light rain had begun to fall. The edge of that ugly storm had already reached Woods Grove. Rather than walk like a lady another twenty feet to a stile, Mercy decided to climb over the split rail fence. There was no one around, after all, and she did need to hurry. The climbing went well enough, but when she jumped down, something caught and her skirt suddenly bound up about her knees.

Her petticoat had hooked over the post. No problem; she could simply climb back up and unhook it. However, climbing a waterlogged fence backwards proved to be more difficult than she had anticipated. Her boots slipped off the rail; there was an ominous tearing sound. For a moment, Mercy dangled like a breathless scarecrow.

Hoofbeats sounded beyond the curve of the road, approaching from the church's direction. Evidently the minister had not been last to leave after all. After scrambling to regain her footing, Mercy backed up against the fence post and assumed a casual air. Her legs, covered solely by pantaloons to the rear, felt chilly. She could only hope that her plight was not obvious to the casual viewer.

She did not recognize the horse, a blaze-faced bay with long legs and big feet, but she took one look at the rider and wished to be invisible. Apparently deep in thought, the English gentleman rose effortlessly to his horse's ground-eating trot. As Mercy had surmised, he was very much at home in a saddle. Perhaps he wouldn't notice a disheveled maiden by the roadside.

Of course, this was a futile hope. He immediately reined in his mount. The horse blew and stamped in protest while its rider stared.

four

With all lowliness and meekness, with longsuffering,
forbearing one another in love.
Ephesians 4:2

"Good afternoon," Mercy greeted formally, then looked away, hoping he would take the hint.

"So it would seem. Better and better," he remarked in beautifully cadenced English. Kicking out of the stirrups, he dropped lightly down, then pulled off his gloves and stuffed them into his waistcoat pocket. He led his horse to the fence and looped the reins around a post. The gelding immediately lowered its head to graze.

Turning to Mercy, the Englishman crossed his arms over his chest, stood with booted feet apart, and looked her up and down. Although he was not a particularly tall man, his was a powerful presence, and his command of the current situation was somewhat daunting. "I searched for you after church, but you had disappeared."

"I. . .I had?" she stammered. The eyes Letty had described as "brooding" were nearly hidden behind long, thick lashes. "I mean, I cannot think why you would. My. . .my father should be along at any moment. He is the blacksmith in town. Perhaps you have seen him, a very *large* man."

"Is he indeed?" His lips twitched. "I have not yet had the pleasure, but I trust you will introduce us, Miss Jones. I hope to meet your entire family."

"How do you know my—"

"Your friend Miss Wentworth told me your name when I asked it, Miss Mercedes Jones."

He had asked? Heart racing, she could only stare helplessly

33

at him. His smile was beautiful. A dimple creased his left cheek, and his teeth were very white. She wished he would leave. . . . She longed for him to stay. . . . Was he aware of her dilemma and laughing at her? Did he intend to harm her in some way? Were she to cry for help, there was no one to hear. Mercy had bested many a boy in a wrestling match, but this was no callow youth.

"Calvin described you to me, and I have carried William's drawing all these years. Although Oscar apprised me of the change in you, I could not have imagined such rare comeliness. "

Mercy could only shake her head. Although her brain could make no sense of his words, warmth trickled down her spine at the sheer beauty of his cultured voice.

"Oscar told me that you awaited my coming, so I have dared to hope." For the first time, doubt tinged his voice. The sparkling smile dimmed. He took a step closer, and Mercy looked into his earnest gray eyes. "About a year ago, I lost touch with Oscar. For weeks now I have been in search of your family. Have you any idea how many Joneses there are in this country?"

The strength drained from Mercy's legs. If not for her snared petticoat, they might have buckled. "Lieutenant Somerville?" she whispered.

"Warren Somerville," he corrected mildly and gave her a little bow. "I said I would come, Miss Jones. I told you that if I lived and God so pleased, I would come to you."

Forgetting her predicament, she searched his face. He was real. Her dream had taken on flesh and blood, breath and warmth—and he was oh, so splendid a man in voice and appearance! "You came!"

His expression brightened again. "You are pleased, then? It has been so long, and for years our sole communication has been second-hand."

"I thought you had forgotten me," she breathed like one in a trance. "A year ago we moved, but only to the next town. There were two blacksmiths in Hood Swamp and none in

Woods Grove, so Pa moved us. Oscar told me you had stopped writing."

"I did not stop. Apparently, we simultaneously changed addresses, and our line of communication was snapped. For the past year I have subsisted on hope: the hope that you would not weary of waiting. As soon as I was able, I came in search of you, Miss Jones. Eventually, I found in Hood Swamp a man who directed me here. I could not, would not rest until I had found you." Those glowing eyes drifted over her face. "Have you forgotten me entirely, my Mercy?"

Before she could answer, a gust of wind caught Mercy's skirts and whipped them forward, abruptly returning her to a rather nippy reality. She flung her hands down, trying to conceal her dilemma. This was no dream. Not even in her worst nightmare could she have invented more appalling circumstances for a first meeting with her ideal man.

After an initial start of surprise, Warren looked away, his lips twitching. "Is there something—uh, may I be of assistance?"

Mercy's voice sounded small. "If you would but turn your back." She fixed her eyes upon the top button of his greatcoat.

"From this angle, it appears that you will need my help. Your garment is firmly caught."

Wide-eyed, she made pushing motions at his chest, shaking her head emphatically. "No, please, I beg of you."

Obediently, he turned his back. With one eye on that broad expanse of gray wool cloth, Mercy desperately struggled to rescue herself and succeeded only in making things worse. The top of the fence post now extruded through a jagged hole in her petticoat. After a moment's fruitless exertion, she ventured, "Perhaps if I could use your arm for support. . ."

Keeping his eyes averted, he extended an elbow for her use. She put one slick-soled boot after the other on the wet rail, using his rock-steady arm as a support, but as soon as she let go with one hand to reach for the petticoat, her left foot slipped and she pitched forward. "Mr. Somerville, could you. . .?" It came out somewhat muffled, since her face was mashed into his coat sleeve.

Before she quite knew what had happened, his arm slipped around her waist and bodily lifted her while he unhooked her petticoat from the post. Gently, he placed her upon the ground and stepped back, holding her elbows. "Are you well?" His voice quivered.

Mercy kept her eyes upon his polished boots and nodded shortly, striving to maintain her last vestiges of dignity. She hauled her shawl back over her shoulders and shivered. Wind whipped and snapped her skirts and his greatcoat.

"Is this your reticule?" As he reached down to pick it up, she turned suddenly, and her hand knocked his top hat into the wet grass. He began to laugh helplessly, head bent, with his hands on his knees.

"I am sorry." Humiliated, cold, and rapidly becoming angry, Mercy picked up the hat and brushed at it.

Warren pulled himself upright, using the fence for support. When Mercy thrust the hat in his direction, he ignored it, lifting her chin with one finger. Startled, Mercy jerked away.

"Mercy, it might have happened to anyone. I will tell no one." His voice held tender amusement.

At that she looked up and wailed, "But *you* will know!"

"Yes, and I shall never forget," he murmured, perusing her face. "I thought I had lost you again, and I nearly despaired. But God caught and held you here until I arrived."

Mercy's anger vanished. Her gaze enmeshed with his until time ceased to exist.

Rain pattered on surrounding shrubbery. Dark spots appeared on the horse's brown hide, and water drops sparkled among Somerville's brown curls. A wind gust lashed nearby treetops into a fury of flailing branches.

His forefinger lightly grazed her damp cheek as he turned away, regarding the skies with a frown. "We must seek cover quickly. This is blowing into a severe squall." He traded her reticule for his hat and returned to his snorting, nervous horse. Despite his marked limp, he leaped easily to the animal's back and held out a hand. "Come, Mercy."

Mercy clutched her shawl at her breast and shivered. Already the hem of her dress was sopping. "I cannot ride with you! What would people say?"

"I care less about talk than about your health and safety. The Colonel can carry two for a short distance. Come; in this matter, I am not to be gainsaid."

So Mercy lifted her arms, and he hauled her up before him to sit sideways on the pommel. Once she was seated, he pulled the folds of his greatcoat around her back. The rain felt like an icy waterfall, but Warren's striped waistcoat was dry. Having little choice, Mercy leaned against him.

She tipped her head back to speak, and her bonnet brim caught him under the chin. "Oh, I do apologize!" she squeaked.

"I would be obliged if you removed that thing. Should you discard it, I promise to replace it."

With her free hand, Mercy tried to untie the sodden ribbon. Giving up, she ripped the limp bonnet from her head and tossed it into the churning morass of a road.

"Much better." He spoke against her ear, and Mercy's eyes widened.

The horse stepped out in a rapid walk, ears swiveling, every muscle strung taut. Occasionally he jumped in place, startled by falling branches and swirling leaves. Mercy was well aware how dangerous a nervous horse could be during violent weather, yet she felt no fear in spite of her precarious seat.

Under cover of the storm, she felt strangely free to say, "Calvin once wrote me that you were betrothed to a lady in England. Whatever became of her?" Warren tipped his head in order to hear her above the pelting rain and howling wind. Did he feel hot shivers when her breath tickled his ear?

Then a terrible thought struck her. Warren had said nothing about his marital state; she had assumed that he was unwed. Was she revealing her heart too freely?

But his answer was forthright and clear. "That lady did me

the favor of eloping with another man while I was at war. Miss Jones, I have written to you many times these five years, but Oscar tells me that you do not receive my letters."

Mercy fixed her eyes upon his lips, only inches from her nose, and saw them tighten when she said, "The last letter I received from you arrived not long after news of Calvin's death from typhus. Shortly thereafter, my father began to collect the family's mail, and I received no further letters. My father forbade me to write. I do recall seeing letters from you addressed to my parents, but I was not, of course, allowed to read them. My mother, I think, rather liked you. She used to chuckle over your letters and give me mysterious smiles."

He glanced down, and their noses nearly touched. "I was devastated by news of your mother's death, and of William's. The world lost a talented young artist and a wealth of mother love when those two passed on."

"And Calvin, too," Mercy said quietly. Again her eyes were drawn to his mouth. "I miss him almost as much as I miss Mama. Having Oscar here is some comfort, for we talk about Calvin at times. Oscar has been a gift from God to our family in countless ways. Before Calvin died, he asked Oscar to come help us."

"I know."

Warren abruptly lifted his face and swallowed hard. Mercy stared at his finely chiseled profile outlined against the background of swirling clouds. This stranger was the man she had idolized since her childhood. His limp was due to the injury for which Calvin had nursed him. His commanding presence was that of a British military officer. The broad forehead, straight dark brows, that long aristocratic nose and square chin, even the dimple that flashed in his clean-shaven cheek whenever he smiled—all belonged to the Warren J. Somerville who had penned her precious letters.

"Warren," she mouthed the name, trying it upon the man himself. Almost she snuggled closer to him, but doubt kept her from displaying her admiration too freely. Now that he had seen her, he might recognize the absurdity of his former attachment to a simple country spinster.

Mercy had been so involved in their conversation that she scarcely noticed the wind's increasing frenzy until the top half of a nearby yellow pine snapped off and crashed to the ground. The Colonel shied violently, and the saddle seemed to drop away from beneath Mercy. "Oh!" She clutched Warren's lapels with both hands, her body dangling in space.

His left arm pulled her back into place upon the saddle's pommel even as he calmly brought his horse under control. "How far is it to your home?"

Mercy peered at her surroundings and pointed through the driving rain. "If you cut across behind the apothecary's stable over there, you will find our barn just beyond."

"Hold tightly." Warren put his horse to a shallow ditch, and again Mercy felt herself airborne. This time she wrapped both arms around Warren's body beneath his coat. His arm tightened its grip until she was barely touching the saddle. Mercy's heart pounded not only with fright, but also with a heady exhilaration unlike anything she had previously known.

Warren allowed the big gelding to canter across the open field, carefully guiding him to the best footing. Chunks of turf flew up behind them only to be dashed back to earth by the deluge of rain.

"Is this it?"

Mercy turned and opened her eyes to see a virtual waterfall cascading from the eaves of her father's barn. A chunk of someone's roof blew past, cartwheeling end over end through the yard. "Yes."

Warren immediately dismounted and helped her down, then hauled open the heavy barn door. Mercy rushed inside and heard hoof beats behind her in the darkness. The door banged shut and cut off much of the noise and light. Wind still howled around the eaves, and rain hammered upon the roof. Mercy's ears felt deadened. A horse snorted somewhere behind her.

"Mercy?"

"I am here." Her eyes began to adjust to dim lighting. Ventilation holes under the eaves allowed a small amount of light to enter. Now amazingly calm, the bay gelding wriggled his lips across the dirt floor, scooping up bits of hay. He lifted his head to answer a welcoming whinny from one of the Jones's workhorses.

"Quiet, Colonel." Warren wrapped a rein around a support post and turned his attention upon Mercy. "I should take you to the house." He settled his greatcoat over the shivering girl's shoulders. In spite of her clammy condition, the coat felt warm and comforting. Her shawl sagged heavily from her elbows.

"I shall be well. You are nearly as wet as I am." As he buttoned the coat under her chin, she looked into his face. Curls lay plastered against his forehead and dangled over his limp collar. His face was shiny wet, and his top hat dripped.

Warren's cold, bare hands cupped her cheeks. His thumbs gently caressed her temples, smoothing back her damp hair. Mercy's knees felt weak.

He sucked in a quick breath. "Mercy, I must say this quickly, before I lose courage. Your father refused to allow me to court you by letter; therefore, at long last, I am here to pursue my suit in person. I cannot tell you the suspense I suffered this past year, wondering if you had married another, praying that God would keep you healthy and free—for me."

Her eyes widened and her lips parted at his forthright declaration. She felt his hands become tense and knew by the look in his hooded eyes that he wanted to kiss her. Her hand lifted to rest upon his striped waistcoat.

The barn door suddenly flew open, letting in wind, rain, and two men. One of them turned back to shove the door closed. "Mercy, is that you?"

"Yes, Pa, I am here and safe," she said as Warren moved away from her. Her voice sounded strangely breathless.

"Thank God! We went in search of you but got only as far as

the gate. Oscar said he saw someone lead a horse into the barn, so we came to see if you had managed to make it home. I cannot recall the last time we had such a storm this time of year."

Then Mercy saw her father's eyes move back and forth between her face and Warren's as though attempting to solve a puzzle. "Who is this?"

"Pa, may I introduce. . ."

Her voice trailed away. She and her father watched as the other two men grasped each other's forearms, then clutched in a sudden embrace. Then they stepped back, still gripping each other's shoulders.

"I knew you would come, Lefty." Oscar Dunn's rich bass voice trembled. "I had just about given up on you. Where have you been?"

Warren could only shake his head. "It has been so long, brother. Far too long."

Mercy saw her father's eyes narrow with sudden comprehension. "That is entirely a matter of opinion. So you decided to honor us with a visit, did you, Mr. Somerville? I thought—I hoped—you had given up."

"The honor in this meeting is entirely mine, Mr. Jones." Warren turned and bowed respectfully. "I would have written to notify you of my impending arrival, but I had lost track of your family's whereabouts. Your daughter informs me that your family relocated to Woods Grove at approximately the same time I moved to a new house. Mail service being what it is, 'tis little wonder that contact was severed."

"That was largely my intent in relocating." The statement fell bluntly from Martin's tight lips. "You have the persistence of a horsefly, sir. Your attachment appears to thrive on air, for I made certain Mercedes had no dealings with you these past four years. What manner of fool would pursue a woman with no encouragement either from her or from her family? Can nothing dissuade you from this most unsuitable match?"

Oscar slowly turned to face his employer. "I must confess that Mr. Somerville asked me to keep him informed about your daughter's life and to remind her frequently of his devotion."

Martin glared at his hired man. "Spy! I hired you only because Calvin requested it, and you abuse my trust in such a manner!"

"I have never abused your trust, sir. You knew about my correspondence with Mr. Somerville, for I informed you of it myself. You never forbade me to speak of him to your daughter." Oscar's rumbling voice held neither malice nor reproof. "Calvin loved him like a brother, as do I. You could not find a finer man should you search the world over."

Warren suddenly sneezed twice.

Martin glowered. "I cannot invite guests to the house, for there is illness in my family, but you are welcome to stay in the barn, Mr. Somerville. I do honor your friendship with my eldest son. Please remain as our guest as long as you wish." It was a grudging but honest invitation.

Warren bowed slightly. "I gratefully accept your kind offer. First, I must stable my horse."

"Oscar, put down straw bedding in the stall next to Caesar's while we dry Mr. Somerville's horse."

"Yes, sir." With respectful obedience, Oscar hurried to do Martin's bidding.

"Mercy, you return to the house."

Mercy gave Warren one shy, apologetic smile and exited the barn. It was still raining heavily, but the wind had abated. "Oh, Lord, do make Pa be kinder to Mr. Somerville!" she begged fervently as she ran across the puddled yard.

❧

After the Colonel had been bedded down, Martin Jones followed Warren and Oscar into Oscar's room at one end of the barn. A small stove pumped out heat, defying the chill that leaked through the walls. Oscar offered the two chairs to his guests while he sat on the cot. Warren sat stiffly, extending his cold hands toward the fire. The cold made his hip ache.

Martin wasted no time. "How long have you been in the States, Somerville?"

"Three years and more."

"Plan to stay?"

"Yes, Lord willing. I have been called to pastor a new church in Beaufort, North Carolina."

"Is that so? You have a hankering to be American?"

"It is done. I pledged my allegiance more than two years ago. I wrote to inform you of the fact."

Martin's bushy brows drew together. "Obstinate young fool. I thought you'd have given up years ago after I refused all those letters. Like to put me in debt if I'd paid all that postage."

"I prefer to characterize the trait as tenacity." Warren smiled. "I would have come here long ago, but completing a degree took longer than I had anticipated. I was obliged to work my way through the last two years. Although I am not a wealthy man, I can provide a comfortable home and modest income."

"Sure you still want Mercedes? Julianne is old enough to wed now, and she's a sight better looking. Better not make your final offer until you've seen my younger girl." Martin tried to joke.

A line appeared between Warren's brows. "I do not choose a mate for outward beauty alone, sir. Mercy is the only woman I have considered taking to wife since the war."

"But you know her only through letters. You'd be wise to discover the girl's faults—which are many—before offering for her," Martin observed wryly.

Although there was wisdom in Martin's advice, Warren inwardly rebelled. "I am here for that very purpose: to become better acquainted with her."

"Tell me more about your employment. If you're a clergy-man, where is your backwards collar?"

"I wear clerical vestments only while I preach, and then only to placate traditionalists. Beaufort Chapel is simply a group of believers from various denominational backgrounds who, since they did not find a place in the existing churches, elected to begin a new church. The building should be in its final stages of construction. My uncle, who owns a plantation near the coast, recommended me for the position of minister. I applied and was accepted. I am expected in Beaufort soon."

"You say you have a house?"

"Yes, the parsonage is supplied. The salary is quite reasonable. We will be comfortable, though not by any means wealthy."

"We. You are mighty sure of yourself," Martin growled, hunkering down in his chair. "I must say, sir, I cannot think well of a courtship that is based upon deceit and conniving. I disapproved your suit in the first place because you are a foreigner, a Brit, an enemy to this country." He lifted a hand to forestall Warren's protest. "Granted, you have switched allegiance, but that, too, is cause for suspicion. A man who will exchange loyalties may well prove unfaithful as a husband."

Warren's jaw tightened. "I can provide character references, sir."

His restrained reply seemed to irritate Martin, who shifted uncomfortably. "Scratchings on paper prove nothing. The girl's grandmother will never consent to her marrying a Brit. My father fought in the Revolution, you see. Ma despises Redcoats. I'm not sure but what one of 'em mistreated her once." With a grunt, he suddenly rose and stated, "We'll send supper out. If you need anything, let me know."

As soon as the door closed behind Martin, Warren jacked off his boots. Water dripped from them onto the packed dirt floor. He glanced around for a good place to set them.

"Try suspending them upside down near the stove." Oscar indicated hooks in the ceiling boards, and the two concocted a way to hang the boots without scratching them.

Warren dropped into the chair, stretched out his aching leg, and wiggled toes that showed through gaping holes in his stockings. "Thanks. Guess I'm still particular about those boots. I've had to lower my living standards some these past years. Arrogance doesn't take a man far when he must work for a living."

Oscar took the other chair. "God has a way of pruning out our faults, Lefty. The years have changed you and me both. The Lord has been pulling out my bitterness by the roots— something like having a tooth drawn. I'm slow to learn, but He is gradually exchanging His patience and peace for my anger and resentment."

"Has it been difficult to work here? Mr. Jones seems rather. . . intolerant." He crossed his arms over his chest and studied Oscar's familiar face.

"He is kinder than he seems, but, yes, at times it is difficult. I cannot explain how it is to pass through life and seldom see an expression of acceptance in another man's eyes. The slaves resent me nearly as much as their masters. There are few other free blacks in the county. Mostly, they keep to them- selves for safety."

"Then where do you fellowship? Is there a worship center for slaves and free blacks?"

"No blacks are allowed in the local church. I hold open-air services at Hooper's plantation for anyone who wishes to attend. Mr. Hezekiah, the schoolmaster in Hood Swamp, brings his family, and Hooper's people come. He is a kind master. Slaves from other plantations are not generally allowed to join us, however. Most masters discourage their people from visiting around. We usually have a white man at our meetings, making sure I don't preach anything dangerous."

"So much for freedom of assembly," Warren sighed. "This was a frequent topic of debate at college. Some slaveholders allow Christian principles to be taught because they believe it will keep their slaves peaceable. Others recognize that Jesus taught the equality of all mankind in God's sight and fear sedition among saints. I do not envy your lot, my friend—and yet I fear the time will come when I, too, must face these issues before my congregation. The clash of principle cannot be avoided forever. I do not fear conflict for my own sake, but I hesitate to expose Mercy to the anger of confronted men."

Oscar folded his arms across his massive chest. "Yet you

knew when you accepted a parish in North Carolina that the issue would certainly arise."

Warren nodded. "I knew. I fear there is still something of the soldier in my nature, for such issues tend to fire my fighting blood. If God so wills, Mercy and I will endure and prevail in His power. We discussed slavery in several of our letters and are of one mind on the issue."

Oscar regarded his friend soberly. "Mercy has her mother's Quaker heart. Confrontation is not her way, but if left to her own judgment, she will unerringly follow Christ's teachings. On the other hand, Mr. Martin and his mother deplore slavery as an institution, yet the idea of black people living in equality with whites frightens them, I believe. Southern Christians, as a rule, prefer to see us as helpless, dependent children whom they must support and protect."

"You say 'if left to her own judgment.' Why?"

"Miss Mercy is not allowed to express her mind freely. The grandmother watches every move these girls make. Mrs. Jones's illness is the only reason you have seen Miss Mercy unchaperoned."

"I see. Although I would not wish ill health upon her grandmother, I am thankful to have experienced the privilege of Mercy's company. She is a treasure, Oscar. I am grateful that you have watched over her all these years, sending other suitors about their business."

"There were few to discourage. It takes a brave man to confront Granny Jones."

"She is worse than her son?"

"Considerably."

"You were always an excellent judge of character. I will trust your opinion on this matter."

"Since you trust my opinion, then I will dare to say: I hope you don't expect perfection in Miss Mercy, my friend. Your long-distance courtship may have led you to idealize the girl. I have observed this family long enough to know that Miss Mercy is quite human."

"Must everyone warn me about her faults? How bad can they be? Is she a licentious woman? A shrew? I know that she has a temper, but so have I." Warren's voice held an edge. "Her letters revealed to me a woman of extraordinary wisdom, courage, and maturity.

"She is wise; yet her wisdom is tempered by a tendency to act on impulse. Her physical courage is matched by emotional uncertainty. She is mature in some regards, yes; but in other ways she is a mere child." Oscar warned.

"I am also aware of her tender heart and loving spirit, and these qualities far outweigh her weaknesses in my eyes." Warren rose to walk across the small room.

With pursed lips and some misgivings, Oscar watched his friend's halting gait. "She knows nothing whatsoever about men, and if her granny has any say in the matter, she never will."

Muscles worked in Warren's jaw, and his shoulders squared in anticipation of armed conflict.

A log shifted in the stove with a muffled thud and a shower of sparks; Oscar picked up the poker and pushed it back into place. "How long do you plan to stay?"

"Until I have obtained permission to wed Mercedes," Warren declared firmly. Then he halted and regarded Oscar with a wry grin, "Or until the end of November. Whichever comes later."

"I have spare blankets, and in the loft there is hay aplenty for your bed. Miss Mercy is a fine cook; we do eat well."

"I shall eat when you eat and work when you work. I shall make myself so agreeable that Martin Jones cannot refuse my suit." He thumped a fist into his palm.

"You would better spend your time praying ceaselessly for miraculous intervention," Oscar remarked with a chuckle.

"Wise advice hereby acknowledged." Smiling, Warren pushed the shutter away from Oscar's window and peered into the gathering darkness. "The storm appears to have subsided. I will go and claim my possessions from the tavern, settle my account, and return directly." Retrieving his boots and coat, he prepared for a short trek to the village tavern.

❧

Later that night, Warren climbed the ladder to the loft. He piled up a prickly hay bed and spread a blanket over it. He had left his boots and topcoat in Oscar's room; now he removed his cravat and waistcoat, deciding to sleep in his shirt and breeches rather than bother with a nightshirt. The blankets were scratchy, and a cold, damp breeze wafted through a crack in the barn wall. He wriggled down into the hay.

The thought crossed his mind that it would be cozy if he had Mercy with him and they were snuggled together beneath the blankets. "Soon," he assured himself with a lazy smile. "I hope."

Looking up toward the barn's dark rafters, Warren prayed softly. "Lord God, thank You for guiding me to her. Thank You for hanging her on a fence where she could not possibly escape my notice. Now, Lord, I humbly ask that You would soften her father's heart toward me. Once again I entreat You: grant me Mercy, Lord!"

five

*"Ye have not chosen me, but I have chosen you, and ordained
you, that ye should go and bring forth fruit, and that your
fruit should remain: that whatsoever ye shall ask of the
Father in my name, he may give it you."*
John 15:16

"Do you think he's awake?"

"Look at the hay stuck in his hair. His hair is curly like
Julianne's."

"But lots shorter. Pa said he was a soldier. I wonder if he's
got scars."

Rasping whispers awakened Warren. He peeked between
his lashes and spotted three young boys near the loft ladder.
One of them had set a lamp on the wooden loft floor. All
three boasted wide blue eyes and freckled noses like Mercy's.
Two had brown hair; the smallest was blond.

Without opening his eyes, he commented, "Does your
father know you have a lantern up here? Could be dangerous.
Why not hang it on that hook up there." He pointed at a support beam.

The largest boy hurried to obey. "We brung your food. It's
in Oscar's room. Mercy sent it over. Are you gonna marry
her? Granny says you're not."

"I do have scars. Want to see?" Warren slowly sat up and
regarded his audience.

Each boy sucked in a guilty gasp, then nodded.

Pulling his shirt off one shoulder, Warren pointed to the
ragged white blotch where no hair grew, high on the right side
of his chest. "The ball came out here," he dropped his shoulder and pointed to the scar on his back, "after entering here.

49

I'm missing a chunk from my shoulder blade, but it doesn't bother me much. The American surgeon dug it out."

"You got shot in the back? Were you running away?"

"No. I had turned my horse in order to shout orders to my men. Want to feel the hole in the bone?"

Three more eager nods, then small, icy hands prodded his shoulder blade. "That musta hurt," the smallest boy opined as they watched Warren pull his braces up over his shoulders.

The oldest boy looked impressed. "I thought Redcoats were all ladies' men, but you're not. Wanna arm wrestle?"

Honored, Warren accepted the challenge. Belly down on the straw, he faced his small opponent. "Need a handicap?" he offered.

"How about you close your eyes and John Wesley sits on your back and tickles you?"

Warren had to chuckle at the plan and the name, but he agreed. The smallest boy straddled his back and picked up a piece of hay. "Ready?"

"Ready!" the opponents both claimed.

Warren let the boy heave and puff awhile before putting his little arm flat on the hay. "Not a bad try. A pity I'm not ticklish."

"No fair! George Fox should win then," the middle boy claimed. "How about two out of three?"

"No, he's way stronger than me. Bet Oscar could whip him, though," George Fox Jones declared.

"You are probably right," Warren admitted. "But I could take all three of you at once."

The words had scarcely left his lips before three boys lit into him and knocked him flat. Laughing, he scrambled out of their clutches. Lifting George over his head, he tossed the boy into the hay. Their brother's screeches of delight caused the other two to beg for similar treatment. Warren was thoroughly warm and awake by the time George announced that he and his brothers must hurry and get ready for school.

Little John Wesley hugged Warren around the waist and

begged him to stay until after school. "Aren't you young for school?" The child looked no older than five.

"Granny says that if he is old enough to get in her hair, he is old enough to go to school," Knox announced. "Teacher says Johnny's smart, and George and me take care that nobody hurts him."

"Please stay, Mister," Johnny begged.

"Mr. Somerville," Warren told them. "And I promise to be here when you come home."

Three wide grins rewarded him. The boys scrambled down the ladder like monkeys and ran shouting toward the house. Warren felt a moment's sympathy for their granny. So much exuberance in one small house must be exhausting for an old lady.

&

When Mercy came in search of the breakfast basket later that morning, she found it inside the barn door, empty. The men must have enjoyed her apple tarts and bacon strips. Warren had slept in the loft, she knew, for her brothers had told her about their early visit in exhaustive detail. Where was he now?

He was not in the barn, she soon discovered. The stalls had been mucked out that morning. Warren's work? Earlier she had spotted him in the yard picking up debris from the storm, looking incongruous though handsome in his stylish clothing. He was not in the forge—a good thing, for he might have been in her father's way there. Where could he be?

At last she found him in the goat pen. Mucking out the pen was usually her chore; after the rain it must be a backbreaking job. The dung cart was nearly full, and deep tracks in the mud told her that Warren had already emptied it more than once.

His back was turned; he did not hear her approach. She stared at him through the rough pole fencing. He wore nicely snug breeches and a tucked white shirt. Elastic braces emphasized his lean, lithe build. The satin gloss of his high black boots lay hidden beneath layers of mud. His sleeves were rolled up, showing surprisingly muscular, hairy forearms.

For a clergyman, he had a very earthly appeal. Mercy wanted to pick up where they had left off the day before, but she did not wish to seem brash. *He is not a stranger; I have known him for years in a way. . .and yet, I have no idea how to behave with him. I cannot treat him like a brother, for he is my suitor. How does one behave with a suitor?*

The only girl she had observed in the act of flirtation was Letty Wentworth. Mercy tried batting her eyes and smiling like Letty, but it did not feel right. Mercy's style with young men tended more toward. . .well, to be honest, her usual style lately was to make excuses and hide away. At one time, she had felt comfortable clapping a fellow on the shoulder and discussing horses or crop prices, but she had abandoned that technique a few years back when, to her chagrin, one burly young farmer had found it appealing.

She could not imagine behaving that way with Warren. He was the first man who had ever made her feel soft, feminine, and. . .well, she had no words to describe the way she'd felt when he clasped her against his chest while they rode through the storm. Whatever that wonderful feeling had been, she longed to experience it again. Wavering, she pulled her long braid over one shoulder and chewed on her lower lip.

"You could frighten a man to death, appearing suddenly that way." Warren leaned an elbow on his shovel and smiled his devastating smile.

Mercy still didn't know what to say. She hadn't intended to startle him. "Mr. Somerville, thank you for cleaning the pen. May I help you?" Perhaps she could impress him with her willingness to work.

When he turned, his weak leg gave way. He grabbed the low roof of the goat shed and steadied himself. "Thank you for the offer, but I am nearly finished. Please pardon my shirtsleeves. I did not expect to be observed here."

Mercy had often seen her father and brothers in their shirtsleeves; she had occasionally even observed them shirtless. Was it bad etiquette for her to see a gentleman thus? Would a lady of refinement hurry away, blushing with shock? His cravat was still tied; nothing except his arms was showing. Uncertain, she just stood there, silent.

"How are your grandmother and your sisters?"

"Not dangerously ill." Mercy had been a rather unsympathetic, distracted nurse to them since his arrival. Warren's inquiry suddenly made her feel guilty. He probably had imagined her soothing their fevered brows with totally unselfish concentration. In actual fact, she was away without leave, having escaped the house while Granny napped.

"I am pleased to hear it. Might you care to join me? 'Twould be easier to talk without a fence between us."

Mercy entered the pen. As she bent over to scratch a kid, one of the does bumped her backside. Laughing, she shoved on the goat's horned head, having a little contest of strength. "So you want war, Magnolia?" After a few hearty pushes, the spotted goat walked away, wearing a satisfied expression.

Warren had stopped shoveling to watch. "They all have names?"

"Oh, yes. Magnolia is mother to Chauncey and Greta. The other two nannies are Wahsoose and Gardenia. I milk them every morning, so they all know me well. Do you like goats?" Chauncey nibbled on the edge of her apron. She tried to shoo him away and still listen politely for Warren's reply.

"I have seldom been near goats until today. I know all about cattle, however. I earned much of my way through seminary working both at a dairy farm and at a livery stable. I could not take a full course load that way, but undoubtedly my health is the better because of it."

Mercy thought he looked magnificently healthy, if, perhaps, a trifle sweaty. "We drink goats' milk because Julianne cannot tolerate cows' milk. We used to have cows, but I cannot say that I miss milking them. The goats are more fun. They have interesting personalities."

Warren smiled, showing her that fascinating dimple once more. "After I am finished here, may I request time for a visit with you? We have much to learn about one another."

"I would enjoy that very much." Mercy felt her heart begin to race in anticipation. Granny was asleep; she could be alone with Warren. Such an opportunity might never again arise.

"Thank you. Would you please collect my coat and waistcoat?" He turned back and scraped the shovel across the earth, smoothing out muddy ridges.

Mercy looked around. "Exactly where did you leave them, Mr. Somerville?"

"On the fence right—" He stopped short, eyes wide, and slowly turned to stare at the high fence posts. "What have I done?" he said on a sigh.

Understanding dawned on Mercy. With a little cry, she rushed into the milking shed and found Gardenia curled up in one corner, contentedly ruminating the sleeve of a fine woolen topcoat. The waistcoat lay nearby, bereft of buttons.

Mercy caught hold of the jacket and pulled it from the nibbling lips. "You dreadful creature; leave it!"

Mr. Somerville spoke from the doorway. "Do you see my gloves anywhere?"

Mercy spotted a man's glove floating in the water bucket. "Here is one." She picked it up by a soggy finger. Wahsoose stood nearby, wearing a thoughtful look. Reading the goat's telltale expression, Mercy felt her heart sink. "I fear the other is lost forever."

She backed out of the shed, clutching the filthy garments to her chest. Showing them to Warren, she asked weakly, "Are they all ruined?"

Warren's scowl relaxed into a wry smile. "If so, I bear the entirety of the blame, for I heedlessly laid them within the goats' reach. I am not such a city boy as to be ignorant of the propensities of goats. I was thoughtless, and now I pay the consequences." He opened the gate and held Chauncey while Mercy exited. She watched him wheel the cart through before quickly closing the gate after himself.

"Do you have another coat? I can replace the buttons on

your waistcoat. We can visit the store and select new ones. I noticed a rip in your shirt, too. I would be happy to care for your laundry and mending."

"Thank you. I would appreciate that. My traveling wardrobe is, of necessity, quite limited." He looked down and lifted his arms slightly, searching for the hole. "I must have torn it while wrestling your brothers this morning." He looked up and grinned. His eyes disappeared into a mesh of black lashes when he smiled.

Now Mercy understood his concern about being caught without his waistcoat: she could see dark hair on his chest through the fine cambric shirt. This encounter did suddenly seem very. . .personal. Her mouth felt dry. "Did the boys bother you?"

"Not at all. I enjoyed them. Mercy, please do not feel that you must impress me in any way. I did not come here intending to look for your faults or for your family's. I wish to know you better in every way, and I want you to know me."

Mercy nodded. "H–how long do you expect to stay in Woods Grove?"

His intent eyes matched the cloudy sky in hue. She hugged his garments tightly against her chest and lost herself in his gaze.

"As long as possible," he murmured. "Your eyes, Miss Jones, remind me of the ocean: deep, blue, and mysterious—dangerous for the unwary. Are you aware of the promises they make?"

Startled and confused, Mercy blinked and took a step back. Dangerous? Whatever did he mean? Perhaps Granny had good reason for never allowing Mercy to be alone with a man. She certainly felt gauche with this one.

Warren must have realized that he had frightened her, for he immediately gave her a formal bow combined with a brotherly grin. "After I dump this load, will you escort me to the store, Miss Jones?"

She nodded jerkily. "For the buttons?"

"Yes. Since I have few garments with me, I do need that waistcoat. Give me time to change, please."

"I—I must fetch a bonnet and gloves." What would Letty say? Mercy could hardly wait to appear before her old friend on Warren's arm.

She took care not to let Granny hear her enter the cabin. Quickly collecting her things, she dashed back outside. Dinner and other responsibilities could wait.

Warren met her in the drive. "I told your father where we planned to go. He was displeased with the idea."

Sure enough, Martin stood in the forge doorway as they passed, his expression stern. "Have you no work to do, girl?"

"Yes, but our goats ate the buttons off Mr. Somerville's waistcoat. I must replace them immediatcly. There is stew for dinner, Pa, and Julianne promised to watch the bread dough for me." Oh, surely he would not forbid this outing!

"It ain't proper, you two goin' off alone. Can't it wait until the boys are home from school?"

"I won't have time later, Pa. I must do the wash this afternoon. Helen and Julianne are not yet well enough to go out."

"Very well then. But mind, don't you linger!" The smith turned on his heel and stalked into the forge.

Warren offered his arm. Mercy shyly rested her fingers on his forearm, but he took her hand and tucked it into the crook of his elbow. Without thinking, she squeezed his arm. He pressed it to his side, pulling her slightly closer.

As they strolled along the town boardwalk, Mercy saw passersby give them curious looks and knew that her entire face must be glowing. She could scarcely contain her pride and excitement. She introduced Warren to several acquaintances as an "old friend of the family."

"I am not so old as that," he whispered as they approached the store. His warm breath on her ear removed her power of speech; she could only smile tremulously in return.

Warren opened the door of Wentworth's and followed Mercy inside. A bell over the door announced their arrival.

The stove in the center of the room radiated heat, yet it did not seem to bother the two gentlemen seated beside it, deeply engrossed in a game of checkers. As always, mixed aromas of spices, molasses, coffee, and cheese tickled Mercy's nose.

There was Letty, dusting shelves behind the store counter. She spotted Mercy and visibly brightened. "Mercy, how good to see you!" Brushing both hands down her apron, she hurried around the end of the counter to greet her friend. "I've been wanting to talk."

Then she noticed Warren. Her green eyes grew wide, and her hand immediately came up to straighten her hair. "I'm so sorry, Mr. Somerville. Have you been waiting long for service?"

"Not at all. We just now entered. Miss Wentworth, it is a pleasure to see you again." He bowed politely.

"How may I help you?" Letty's long eyelashes fluttered. She often, even at work, wore fashionably low-cut gowns. This had never bothered Mercy before, but today she wanted to pull a sack over her friend's head and shoulders. She fiercely resented any other woman displaying her charms to Warren. He should see and admire only Mercy, ever. But what could he see of her figure while she wore this frightful gray shift? Not a thing. Next to Letty, Mercy looked about as shapely as a bale of hay.

Mercy linked her arm back through Warren's and pressed close. She felt his muscles tighten and saw him give her a startled glance. "Mr. Somerville needs new buttons for a waistcoat."

Letty looked from Mercy to Warren. "I was unaware that you two were acquainted."

"This is the Mr. Somerville who was friends with my brother Calvin during the war. You remember, don't you? I showed you a few of his many letters to me." There was more than a hint of smugness in her voice. She could not help recalling how Letty had giggled when Mercy talked about her British soldier. "He promised years ago to come visit our family, and now he is here. Is it not exciting? He is staying with us until he begins his new ministerial position at Beaufort, over on the coast."

Mercy felt warm and knew that she was talking too much and too fast, but she could not stop. The warm, solid feel of Warren's arm against her body seemed to delete intelligent thought from her mind. "I was thinking that perhaps bone buttons would be nice for the waistcoat."

Letty brought out a display of buttons, listened to Mercy's mindless chatter, and studied the way her friend was plastering herself against the handsome Englishman's arm. Warren made no attempt to extricate himself; he seemed somewhat preoccupied in his mind.

When the buttons had been selected, wrapped, and paid for, Warren opened the door for Mercy. She stepped outside, waving airily to her old friend. "We will see you later, Letty. Thank you."

"Miss Wentworth," Warren nodded politely.

They walked along the street in silence for a few minutes. When they reached the lane, Warren said softly, "Miss Jones, I believe we need to talk."

Mercy increased her pace, forgetting about his limp. He sounded upset. Why would he be upset? It wasn't as though she had done anything shocking. She had seen other women hang on men's arms, although this was the first time she had tried it.

He caught her arm and brought her to a stop in the middle of the lane. "What was that all about?"

"What was what about?" Mercy felt blood rush into her cheeks.

"You understand my meaning."

Mercy began to tremble. She could only stare at him dumbly.

"If you intended to draw my attention to yourself, I can assure you that your efforts were successful. You also drew the attention of every other person in that store."

Mercy could not speak for fear of bursting into tears. She attempted to breathe deeply and calm herself, but her breath kept catching. "I am sorry."

"Oh, Mercy, my dear girl," Warren sighed. His hands lifted close to her shoulders, then dropped helplessly to his sides. "How you tempt me!"

"I do?" she blurted, brightening. Then her face fell. "Is that bad?"

A smile flitted across his face, drawing her attention to his mouth. "In some ways, yes. I have no right to touch you, and yet you entice me to do it every moment."

"You held me tightly yesterday while we rode your horse."

His face reddened, and he looked away. "That was an extreme circumstance, but you are right: I did take advantage of it, and I apologize. I will also admit that, had your father not entered the barn when he did, I would likely have taken advantage of that moment as well. God intervened, and I am thankful that He did. I want our relationship to be entirely pure, wholly pleasing in God's eyes. My dear, we must be careful that our love is founded not upon desire, but upon mutual respect and unselfish regard. Please do not tantalize me again as you did today until after we are wed."

"I did not understand that it was wrong." The knot in Mercy's throat choked her. "I will—I will be good."

≈

Warren prayed while he worked alone in the barn each morning and evening that week, asking the Lord for patience, wisdom, and clarity of thought. He sincerely wished to make a deep and lasting emotional and spiritual bond with his chosen future wife. Daily, hourly, he begged God to grant him Mercy, yet he resolved to relinquish his love if it ran contrary to God's will. He felt as though his heart were tearing in two when he considered the fact that Martin Jones seemed no nearer to granting permission for the match.

"Yet I know that You have placed Mercy under her father's care, and I must respect his wishes. Please, please, soften his heart toward me, God. Teach me how to honor him and earn his favor."

Mercy's grandmother was still weak, although recovering from her illness, so Warren had not as yet even laid eyes upon her. But her illness did mean that Mercy and Warren were free to talk and work together. Mercy had begun to relax and behave more normally in his presence, especially when her brothers, her father, or Oscar chaperoned them; yet Warren gradually became aware that Mercy would no longer directly meet his eyes and that she seemed to avoid touching him.

It must be that she wishes to honor my request to keep our relationship pure, he mused, watching as she kissed Johnny's scraped elbow and gave the whimpering boy a tender hug. This mild, sunny fall afternoon she wore a faded blue dress that complemented her eyes. Warren noted that she seemed embarrassed about its frayed hem and cuffs, but he thought it the most flattering garment she had worn to date. It looked soft. . .and she looked soft in it.

Consoled, Johnny hopped down from his sister's lap and scampered off, his small hound at his heels. Mercy turned back to peeling apples. Warren studied her curving pink lips and had a sudden urge to skin his own elbow. *Perhaps I should not have pressed the point about temptation quite so emphatically.*

He leaned back in the porch chair and crossed one ankle over his knee. "May I assist you?"

"Perhaps when it comes time to chop the apples," she allowed with a smile.

"I feel useless."

"You are hardly that. Even Father has mentioned how hard you work. He appreciates your help around the place. Every fence mended, every tool sharpened and cleaned, every beast well fed and groomed. You are scarcely ever still."

"It is the least I can do. Miss Jones, do you know how lovely you are?"

He watched the color creep into her cheeks as she shook her head. For an instant, her eyes lifted to meet his, and he read in them her pleasure at his remark. "No one has ever thought me lovely before. There is nothing special about the way I look."

"If that is true, why do I delight in looking upon you?" Warren found himself at a loss to expound upon her beauty. The way she held herself with dignity and poise—her graceful movements enthralled him. Her skin was freckled, yes, but it glowed like fine ivory, smooth and soft. Her hair reminded him of a brook: shining, brown, and sparkling with flecks of gold; he longed to see it loose and flowing over her shoulders. Her body was supple, strong, and curved in all the right places. And her eyes never failed to captivate him, changing as they did from pacific blue to stormy slate depending upon her moods. She had a way of sweeping her lashes up to sneak glances at him that invariably tied his middle into knots.

He saw her lips curve into a tiny smile. "I cannot answer that question, sir. Why do you?"

"Because I love you so dearly, I imagine," he answered softly. "Mercy, do you think it too soon for me to approach your father about our marriage? Or perhaps I should ask if you still care for me now that we have met and become better acquainted. My love for you has redoubled in intensity these past days; no—even that description is inadequate. I simply cannot imagine life without you, my dearest Mercy." His voice became strained as he continued, "Please do not make me wait any longer. Do you care for me?"

"Yes, Mr. Somerville." Her hands became still, holding a half-peeled apple over the pan. "I do believe Father is becoming impatient that you have not already approached him. He talked with me the other night. So did Granny."

"And?" Warren scooted to the edge of his chair.

She chewed on her lower lip, studying the apple in her hand, and shook her head. "I do not know what he will say to you. I am. . .I am afraid," she whispered. "Granny is terribly against the entire idea."

"Will you pray with me now, before I speak to him?"

Mercy nodded. Warren simply closed his eyes and spoke.

"Lord God, the time has come when we will discover if our marriage is in Your plan. You know my wishes and desires on the matter, for I have certainly spoken of them often—and it seems that Mercy's wishes are in accord with mine. Lord, You have promised to grant us the desires of our hearts when we seek Your face and follow Your paths—right now, we lay before you our—our vital petition and ask that You will bless it with Your approval, and with the favor of Martin Jones. Nevertheless, not our will but Yours be done."

A tear trickled down Mercy's cheek. "Are you still afraid, my dear?" Warren asked, feeling helpless. If only her chair were closer to his, he could at least pat her hand.

She shook her head. "It was. . .your prayer. When you pray, I feel God here with us. I do believe it will work out well after all."

⁂

Warren found Martin Jones in the barn. He had just returned from a delivery run and was stabling Caesar and Cleo. Warren silently helped him remove the horses' harnesses and brush them down.

"Something on your mind, Somerville?" Martin asked in his gruff way.

Warren straightened and looked the older man in the eye. "Yes, sir, there is. I wish to request your permission to marry your daughter and your blessing upon our union."

"Do you now?"

Warren pulled a bundle of papers from an inner coat pocket. "I have here numerous references, transcripts, and citizenship papers should you wish to look into my background, Mr. Jones."

Martin accepted the bundle and riffled through it. He stopped to scan a reference from a college professor who described Warren as a man of "impeccable integrity." Shaking his head, he returned the papers to Warren. "Are you runnin' for governor or are you proposin' marriage? Why're you tryin' to impress me with all this stuff?"

Warren turned brick red, but stood tall and proud. "I want you to understand that I will do my utmost to give your daughter a happy life. I want you to know that I am a man who would never be unfaithful to my wife. I—"

Martin interrupted. "Fine, fine; I take back all my doubt about your loyalty. What I still don't understand is why you want to marry Mercy. She's passing fair—got her grandmother's shapely figure and her mother's pretty face—but she's got my freckles and hair. She's got education enough— Nancy insisted on that—but her best talent is hard work. A fancy fellow like you don't need a workhorse for a wife; you need a decoration for your parlor. I still think you oughta take a gander at Julianne before you make your final decision."

"Have you any real objection to my suit?"

"Nothing to speak on. You got to pass muster with her granny before all's said and done."

"Then I have your blessing?"

Martin paused, then nodded shortly.

"And I may approach your daughter with my proposal?"

The father studied him through narrowed eyes. "Make it quick. I'll be watching you."

❧

"Granny says I am no fit wife for a minister. I do love Jesus and wish to serve Him, but at times I fail Him completely." Mercy was on her last apple, peeling quickly with nervous fingers. "Are you sure you really want to marry me? I don't feel worthy of you." Her voice faded to a whisper. Evening shadows were deepening, and Warren's face was shadowed. She hoped he could not see the tears that kept escaping down her cheeks.

"Mercy, you are a woman of rare inner quality. I know this from your letters, from the testimony of your family and friends, and from my own observation. In my wife, I desire a friend and companion as well as a lover, housekeeper, and mother of our children. I am certain you will suit me in every respect. I believe we will complement one another with our respective strengths and weaknesses. I need you, Mercy. If I lacked the hope that you will soon be with me, helping and encouraging me, I would feel intimidated by the prospect of pastoring the Beaufort church."

Surprise brought her eyes back to his face. "But why? You seem to me completely fitted for the position. What could be lacking?"

"I fall short in many ways, Mercy. Should you choose to marry me, I know you will quickly discover my faults. I have them in abundance; make no mistake. At times I wonder why God would call me to the ministry when so many men are better suited to the occupation. There is no accounting for the choices of others, you see. I am the man He has chosen, just as you are the woman I have chosen."

His beautiful voice never failed to melt her heart, and the idea of being needed appealed deeply. Mercy longed to be needed not just for her ability to work, but for herself.

"If you truly need me, then I will marry you, Warren Somerville. I am honored by your request." Her voice trembled slightly, but she was amazed by her ability to speak at all when so much emotion filled her heart.

Joy vibrated in his voice. "Thank God!" He struggled to rise from the bench—Mercy hurt for him every time she saw him wrestle with that leg. "Is your grandmother yet well enough to see me? I have been wishing to meet her, and your father tells me I must have her approval before our marriage can proceed."

Anxiety puckered Mercy's forehead. This bridge might be the most hazardous of all to cross. "She is demanding to meet you. Please, be—be warned that she is. . .strong in her opinions."

He nodded. "Oscar warned me. I believe I will survive her scrutiny. I have an aunt whom we often called Medusa, for her gaze surely reduced us children to stone."

Mercy dropped the last apple into the large pan and stood up. "I am going in now. It would be best if you wait until tomorrow to meet Granny. I will arrange a time to suit you both."

"Very well. I am also looking forward to meeting your sisters. I believe I once saw—is it Helen?—peering at me through a back window."

Mercy smiled. "Yes, the girls are eager to meet you. Don't expect Helen to talk; she is exceedingly shy. Granny is likely to dominate the conversation anyway."

"May I carry those apples in for you? That pan looks heavy."

Mercy could scarcely see his face, for darkness had fallen quickly. She shifted the burden to rest on her hip. "Thank you, but I can manage. You should not come inside; Granny would scalp me if you surprised her that way. I will bring supper to you and Oscar shortly, and I will bake a pie just for you two."

"May I have cream with it?"

"Certainly. Goat cream, that is."

Warren stepped closer to her. "Mercy?"

"Yes?" She turned to him, feeling braver now that he could not read her expression. Oh, but he was good to look upon. She could discern his outline still, the proud set of his shoulders, the curly hair that needed cutting.

"May I kiss you?"

He touched her hand, and she nearly dropped the pan. "But you said—"

"Disregard what I said the other day—at least for the moment. Mercy, I have been longing to kiss you since the moment I saw you dangling from that fence post. It is dark; no one will see. We are engaged now."

His fervent plea shook her, quite literally. She could not stop shaking. After her recent talks with Granny, she was afraid to let Warren see how intensely she desired his kiss.

He interpreted her silence as refusal.

"I know that I am bold to ask before we are wed." He sounded humbled. "I would not wish to embarrass you. I had thought you might wish to be kissed. I presumed too much. Forgive me."

His dejected tone was more than she could bear. Forgetting her resolve for one crucial moment, Mercy set the pan down, rose on her tiptoes, and pressed her lips against his, warm and promising. Warren's arms instantly encircled her; he drew her closer and closer.

"I wondered what might be going on over here in the dark," Martin Jones's dry voice startled them apart. "Reckon it's a good thing I came to see. Mercedes, you git on in the house and fix supper. Girl, I oughta give you a whuppin' here and now! Don't you say nothin'—just git on inside."

Mercy picked up her heavy pan and scooted into the house, where she immediately set to work. Sobs ached inside her chest until late that night when, lying awake amid the snores of her siblings, she released them in a torrent of silent tears. *Oh, what must he think of me? There was nothing pure or godly about that kiss—that fire I felt, was it evil? Is this what it means to burn with lust? He told me not to tantalize him, but I can't seem to help it! Everything within me cries out for his touch, his kisses. Oh, Lord, help me! Show me what to do.*

six

He who guards his lips guards his life,
but he who speaks rashly will come to ruin.
Proverbs 13:3

"Save me!"

Warren turned just in time to see two little bodies racing toward him. An instant later, Johnny slammed into him, still shrieking. "He's gonna kill me!" Small, constricting arms wrapped around his legs.

"Why are you wearing my hat?" Warren retrieved his top hat from the little boy's head and quickly donned it.

George pulled up short, glaring. "He stole it from me!"

"Odd; all this time I thought it was my hat."

"We found it on a hook in the barn. Didn't know it was yours," George explained lamely.

"So it became yours by right of discovery, I suppose. It fits Johnny very ill. I am surprised he could see well enough to run."

"Your head is bigger than his."

"One would hope. In future, leave my possessions alone. Hear me?" The two boys nodded soberly.

Softened by their chastened expressions, Warren peeled Johnny off his legs and put a hand on each boy's back. "Would you escort me into the house? I am invited to be introduced to your grandmother today."

"Granny says Pa ought to run you off our property because Grandpa fought your kind in the Revolution. She says she can't raise all of us alone without Mercy's help, and Pa had better not expect it—"

"Why not let Granny tell me these things herself if she so

67

chooses?" Warren suggested, interrupting Johnny's report. "Some of her sayings may not be intended for my ears. Tell me about school. What did you learn this week?"

Each of them scraped his boots at the cabin door.

"I know all my alphabet now," Johnny announced, his round freckled face beaming.

Warren ruffled the boy's hair. "Excellent."

"Baby stuff. I'm learning fractions and second declension nouns," George growled. "Did you have to take Latin?"

"In plenitude. Hebrew and Greek, too. Frankly, I have already forgotten most of it—but I suppose it would come back to me should I need it."

George shoved open the door and led the way inside. "Granny? Mr. Somerville is here to see you."

Warren hung his hat on a wall peg. The room was dimly lit. Mercy was working at the fire, stirring a kettle of stew. A younger girl lay near the fire, her shoulders wrapped in a blanket. Another girl played on the floor with a rag doll. All three stared at Warren.

A woman rose from her spinning wheel. "Bring him over here, George Fox."

Granny Jones's voice was much stronger and deeper than Warren had expected. Instead of a wizened crone in a rocking chair, he discovered a stately woman. Few wrinkles marred her pale face, though her brown hair was streaked with white. She stood only two inches shorter than Warren's five foot nine. Her shoulders were square, her back was straight, and her limbs were wiry and strong.

"Get on with you, boys. Go help your Pa in the forge. Mercy will call you when dinner is ready."

Fixing bright, cold blue eyes upon Warren, the woman said, "I am Eliza Jones, but everyone calls me Granny whether they're blood kin or not. So you are the cause of all this excitement, eh? You ain't so very tall. Mercy should have a large man like I did, since she takes after me. You wouldn't guess it, but I looked just like her when I married my Amos."

Warren bowed and said truthfully, "And you are still a handsome woman, Mrs. Jones. It is my pleasure to make your acquaintance."

"Hoity-toity, now ain't we fine? Such high-falutin' manners and fancy talk! Why don't you find yourself a woman of your own kind and leave our Mercedes alone?"

Forget decorum. Warren crossed his arms over his chest and returned, "Why don't you accept facts and make the best of the situation? Mercy has accepted my proposal with her father's blessing, and I fully intend to wed her."

Warren returned glare for glare. Mercy, Julianne, and Helen sat still, their eyes wide with suspense.

Then Granny looked away, scowling. "My boy Martin always was a fool. A Brit! Never thought I would see the day. I'm a sick woman. May not live till the wedding day at any rate." She resumed her seat at the wheel and began to separate wool strands with her long fingers.

Warren suppressed a smile. He had seen grudging acceptance in the woman's blue eyes, although she would never admit that she had met her match.

"I wish you would lie down again, Granny. You do look pale," Mercy said, appearing at Warren's side. "Granny's heart is not strong," she informed him quietly.

"Leave me be, child. If I spend another minute lyin' down, I'll lose my mind. So tell me, Mr. Somerton: when is this wedding to take place?"

"Somerville," Mercy corrected quickly. "Warren Somerville."

Granny looked cross. Her hands flew more rapidly than her tongue, and her foot pushed the treadle. Thump, thump, thump. Coarse woolen thread filled the spindle. Mercy moved behind Warren and collected something from a cupboard. Her skirts brushed against his legs in the confined space.

"Somerville. Hmph! Ridiculous name. I was fifteen when I married my Amos, and birthed Martin Luther the year after. We had seven children, but only Martin lived to marry and have his own brood. Nancy, his wife, died in childbed. I certainly never did that."

A difficult comment to dispute. Though Warren wondered how the topic of a wedding date had been so thoroughly lost, he listened politely.

"Nancy was a weak little thing. Slipped and fell on the ice, went into labor far too soon, and we lost her. That was only weeks after young William Penn Jones was buried; he died of the measles. Nancy never should have had so many babies. Julianne is like her. That one should marry a fine gentleman like you who could take her to the seashore and pamper her. Mercy is made for hard work and childbearing. She should marry a farmer. One started to come around a month or two ago, but she had no use for him. Have yourself a seat, young man."

Warren obediently pulled up a chair and sat down near Granny. Mercy returned to the fireside with a stack of bowls and began to ladle out possum stew.

The door opened, and Johnny entered, his face long and sad. His beagle followed him inside and laid its head on Warren's knee, wagging a busy tail. Warren scratched its soft ears and remarked, "I admire Mercy's diligence and cooking skills. I like children and hope to have several. Mercy suits me perfectly."

Granny lifted a sardonic brow in his direction. "One of *those,* are you? I'll give the girl a good talking to, I aver. She needs a chance to change her mind." Her voice was too low to reach Mercy's straining ears.

Warren's remark had been straightforward. What possible double meaning could the woman have read into his words?

Johnny approached and leaned against Warren's shoulder. Without a thought, Warren picked up the small boy and let him sit on his knee. Evidently hungry for affection, Johnny snuggled against his shoulder and sighed.

Granny cogitated aloud. "Now I better understand your choice of bride. Julianne would not suit your purposes. So you want a brood of younguns, do you? I'll keep that in mind.

Now when did you say you plan to marry?"

Warren said only, "Before Christmas."

"You are wise. Traveling on winter roads in these parts is nigh impossible. Best head for the coast before the real cold sets in. I'll arrange the wedding ceremony and dinner. We will invite a good number of friends, perhaps fifty. This is the first wedding in our family since Martin and Nancy tied the knot."

"But Granny, we must consider your health. I do not think you should attempt a large wedding party," Mercy blurted out.

"Nonsense. You will do most of the work, and we'll keep the expense to a minimum by making it a carry-in dinner. You may wear my wedding gown; you would never fit into your mother's."

Warren quickly interjected, "I plan to order a gown for her in Beaufort. She can tell me what she wants, and I will purchase the gown as a wedding gift."

"Hope you don't plan on satin and lace. The girl would look absurd in finery. Good, plain gray wool would suit her best and wear longest."

"Mercy may choose whatever she desires. If wool is her choice, then wool she will have." Warren spoke pleasantly, his eyes drifting to Mercy, who was setting bowls around the pine table. She glanced up and met his gaze. He was satisfied to see anticipation in her eyes. Somehow he sensed that he would not be ordering gray wool.

&

"My, but your time here passed quickly. Seems as though you just arrived. Have you and Miss Mercy set a wedding date?" Oscar inquired, bending over the Colonel's front hoof. A breeze from the smithy's open doorway cooled his sweating cheeks.

Placing a hand on the gelding's high withers, Warren answered, "December seventeenth. Three and a half weeks from today. I must return here for the wedding."

"Why do you not marry first, then travel to Beaufort? Under the circumstances, I am certain your employers would understand the delay." Oscar clipped off overgrown hoof with a pair of nippers. Johnny's beagle immediately picked up the chunk of hoof and ran off to gnaw on it.

Warren cast a glance over the Colonel's back at his future father-in-law, who was working over the forge. Although Martin seldom joined their conversations, he could hear almost every word. "Yes, but Mrs. Jones will not hear of moving up the date. I did promise Mercy a wedding gown, and her grandmother desires a large wedding party. These things cannot be obtained or arranged at short notice, and I must appear in Beaufort without further delay. I am already somewhat later than I had originally indicated—although I did write my uncle an explanation."

"What are your transportation plans? Roads in this state are mighty primitive."

Warren frowned. "I had considered purchasing a vehicle in Beaufort and driving it here for the wedding, but perhaps it would be best to abuse it on the roads as little as possible. Do you know anyone in Woods Grove with a carriage they might sell?"

"I do." Martin Jones broke in.

Warren watched sparks fly as the older man hammered on a red-hot axle. "Do you, sir?" he ventured to ask.

"I got a carriage what needs a buyer. I'll sell cheap. You won't find a better buy in town. Just what you need for a family."

Oscar gave his employer a sharp glance in passing, then quickly pumped the bellows up and down, holding a partially formed horseshoe in the forge's hot flame until it began to glow red. He did not so much as glance Warren's way; nevertheless, his friend received the message.

"I was thinking along the lines of something new, sir."

"You ain't even seen it yet," Martin gave him a sour look. Leaving the glowing metal bar on his anvil, he beckoned. "Follow me."

Warren obeyed. Martin led the way to an open-sided shed

behind the barn and hauled back burlap sacking to reveal a carriage. . .or was it a small hearse? Cobwebs draped the ancient vehicle's seats and dashboard. Its black and yellow paint was bubbled and peeling; rust darkened its every exposed metal piece. A mouse slipped through a crack in the side door, dropped to the ground, and skittered past Warren's boot.

"They don't make 'em like this anymore. She's one of a kind."

Mercy's father appeared to be serious. Swallowing a sarcastic remark, Warren scrambled for an excuse. "I was thinking of something lighter—"

"Needs a mite of fixing up and she'll be better than new. I hate to part with her, but at least she'll be going with a member of the family." Martin patted the cracked leather driver's seat, and dust billowed. "I'll spruce her up and oil her joints before the wedding. You'll need a pair of sturdy horses; I know just the pair you're lookin' for, and I can get them at low cost."

Warren found it difficult to believe that Martin was sincere, but he did not wish to antagonize his prospective father-in-law. He must have stammered something satisfactory, for Martin looked pleased when they returned to the forge.

Oscar looked from Martin to Warren and lifted a questioning brow. Warren raised both eyebrows in return and turned his palms upward.

&

That afternoon, Martin closed the forge early and set off to make deliveries, leaving Oscar free to visit with Warren. "He has a good heart," Oscar tried to explain as the two young men swept and straightened the smithy. "I can't imagine which horses he has in mind for you. If they match the coach, they may already be in their graves."

Warren chuckled ruefully. "If he weren't Mercy's father, I would know how to refuse. Should I purchase this coach, it is unlikely that I could afford another for some time."

"I will do what I can to make it sound and safe."

"I appreciate that offer more than words can express. Are you planning to stay here?"

Oscar paused and leaned on his broom. "I've been thinking and praying on that question. I hate to leave the master short of hands, but George and Knox will soon be old enough to take on more duties. The boys avoid work now, but if Miss Mercy and I both leave, their Pa will likely force them to take up their proper load of chores. It may be best for the family."

"Any time you need a place to stay, my home is your home. Want a job? I'll need a driver for that coach—and someone to repair it when it breaks down."

Oscar drew a deep breath and exhaled on a sigh. "I believe I'll accept that offer, Lefty. When Jonesy died, I thought I would never know another such man. I was wrong. Your friendship renews my hope."

"God can work in any man's heart, Oscar. You know better than anyone how much work He had to do in me. At times, I wish He would finish the job and have done with it."

Oscar's deep laugh resounded from the shop's rafters. He opened his mouth to reply then stopped short, gazing over Warren's shoulder.

Warren turned to see Mercy and Johnny in the open doorway. Mercy smiled timidly, uncertain of her welcome. "May we join you?"

"But of course!" both men replied. Warren stepped forward to escort her inside. Johnny bounced past with his dog at his heels. "Whatcha doing, Oscar?"

"Cleaning up. You want to help?"

"Can't. Granny told me to stick with Mercy. That's why I'm not at school. I've got to be her 'chap-who-owns,' or something like that."

Warren could not restrain a chuckle. "Only until we are married. Then I shall be the chap who owns her."

Mercy wore a grayed straw bonnet that appeared even older than the one she had discarded during the storm. Mannish boots peeped from beneath her dress's frayed hem, and a faded shawl draped her shoulders. "Pa tells me you are leaving in the morning." She looked wistful.

"Yes. They expect me in Beaufort by the end of the month. Allowing for travel time, I should just about make it. Oscar re-shod the Colonel today, and I have packed my bag. When I return, I shall bring your gown. You have not yet told me your preference. I know nothing about dress patterns or measurements or fabrics."

"I came to ask if you would accompany Johnny and me to the store. Granny needs a few items. Perhaps I may study a fashion book and look at fabrics while we are there."

She lifted hopeful blue eyes, and Warren felt himself melt inside. "I can think of nothing I would enjoy more. Let me finish here, and—"

"You go on. I can handle this, Lefty." With a rather paternal smile, Oscar waved them away. "Better get on the job, chap-who-owns," he reminded Johnny.

Warren offered his arm. Blushing, Mercy laid her fingers upon it. Warren wondered if she were remembering their first trip to the store.

Once again, Letty Wentworth hurried to serve them. She seemed slightly reserved in her greeting. Although she and Mercy had seen one another at church, they had not spoken in weeks. Johnny made a beeline for the rows of candy jars.

"Letty, have you heard the news? Mr. Somerville and I are engaged to be married." Mercy's voice was hushed, as though she scarcely believed her own words.

"Then it is true? I had heard rumors, but I could not. . .I—I am sure that I wish you joy," Letty stammered. Turning a direct gaze upon Mercy, she clearly demanded an explanation at some future date.

"We wish to look at sugar and tea and fashion books and fabrics," Mercy said. "For a wedding gown. I mean, the sugar and tea are for Granny, but the other is for my gown. Warren wishes to order it for me."

"Of course," Letty said weakly.

Warren had actually intended to order the gown in Beaufort, but he held his tongue. Mercy was nervous enough already. He watched Letty direct his betrothed toward a shelf of silks and laces. Miss Wentworth's work gown was of finer quality than Mercy's Sunday best, he realized. How would Mercy look in a pretty new gown?

He strolled to the counter and joined Johnny. "What is your favorite?"

The boy pointed to the peppermint sticks. "What's yours?"

"I like licorice and horehound. It does look good, doesn't it?"

Wandering back toward the stove, he observed the day's checkers match, taking occasional glances toward the corner where his flushed and happy lady pored over a book and fingered fabrics. Her growing excitement pleased him. She began to resemble a joyful bride. For the past few weeks— ever since their engagement was settled, in fact—she had seemed restrained and unnatural in his presence. Had her father chastised her for allowing him that kiss?

That kiss. The memory set Warren's pulses racing. He swallowed quickly and looked away. *Three and a half weeks from now. . .*

"The dressmaker will be in Monday. That gives us plenty of time to decide exactly what you want," Letty announced. Apparently, she was starting to enjoy her role as friend of the bride.

The two young ladies approached Warren, smiling. Mercy's eyes looked slightly anxious, he thought. Reaching out, he took her hand and squeezed it. "Did you find what you want?"

Her fingers curled lightly around his. "I know that you had planned to order the gown in Beaufort, but Letty says it would be best if I have it fitted."

Letty pitched in. "It would be dreadful to have a wedding gown that did not fit well. Our dressmaker is excellent. She will have Mercy's dress ready by mid-December, I am certain."

"Very well. I will pay in advance. If more is due, I will set-tle with your father upon my return." Warren extracted several gleaming coins from his purse and laid them upon the counter. Johnny stood on tiptoe beside him, straining to watch the transaction.

Letty hurried around the counter to take up her role as shopkeeper. Upon a closer look at the coins, she gave a little chuckle. "I am certain this will be sufficient—unless Mercy desires a ten-foot train of Brussels lace and pure silk. Miss Lucy Netterby's rates are quite reasonable. Mr. Somerville, I hate to disappoint you, but you may not see even the picture of Mercy's chosen dress, for it would be unlucky, and we wish to surprise you."

Warren was pleased to note that Letty's smile held none of its former flirtatiousness. She was evidently delighted by her friend's good match and would not attempt to lure him away.

"Did you order a new bonnet?" he asked his fiancée.

Mercy nodded. "I can wear this old one until Miss Netterby comes."

"If there is anything else you need, please order it." He looked directly into her eyes until she nodded. Glancing at Letty, he enlisted her aid. "Miss Wentworth, see that she is properly fitted out, will you?"

"Indeed I shall," Letty declared with a decided nod. "Nothing but the best for our Mercy."

"Before we go, I would like a dozen horehound and pep-permint sticks," Warren added, nodding toward the glass jars. He heard Johnny's gasp of delight. Two ladies entered the store as Letty wrapped the candy in brown paper and entered it on Warren's account. Warren hefted the sacks of sugar and tea under one arm and accepted the candy parcel.

After asking the new customers to wait a moment, Letty followed her friends to the door. "I shall see you in a few weeks, Mr. Somerville! Congratulations, and God's richest blessings upon you both." She gave Mercy a quick hug before returning to duty.

As they walked along the muddy boardwalk, Warren awarded a peppermint stick to Johnny for "being a fine chaperone." Pleased, the boy skipped ahead, picking up assorted objects, and occasionally secreting them in his pockets.

"Once last summer he brought home a baby snapping turtle in his pocket," Mercy remarked. "It lived through the experience, surprisingly enough. Thank you for buying him the candy."

"Would you like a piece?"

"No, thank you. I could carry one of those sacks."

"No, thank you. They are merely awkward, not heavy."

After a short pause Warren remarked, "Miss Wentworth evidently thinks highly of you."

"We have been friends for many years. She and her brother attended school with us in Hood Swamp, for there was no school here in Woods Grove until recently."

"I seem to recall a story about you whipping a boy at school. Does he still live nearby?"

Mercy gave him a horrified look. "I never told you that! Was it Calvin?"

"You told Calvin in a letter, which he read aloud to me. Did this boy admire you?"

"If he did then, he does no longer. He married an heiress from Savannah, and I do not envy her. Lemuel Griffith is handsome but very selfish."

"Is he now? I have a tendency toward selfishness, myself. I wish to keep you to myself and never again share you with anyone, yet I know that this cannot be." He sighed melodramatically.

Mercy smiled, clasping her hands before her. "Indeed, not! Granny will be watching for me. I have many chores waiting at home. The older boys will be out of school, and—"

"Can you not neglect your chores this once and spend the afternoon with your fiancé?" Warren pleaded. "It is a fine afternoon, and I am leaving early in the morning. Once I return you to your granny, I am unlikely to see you again.

They had better begin to learn how to survive without you, Mercy mine."

Mercy looked up at scattered, rushing clouds. "I would not call it 'fine,' but at least it is not raining. Did you wish to take a walk?"

"I would enjoy that exceedingly. However, I would like to deliver these packages first."

Naturally, the idea of a walk appealed to Mercy's brothers, and their grandmother encouraged all of them to join their sister's late afternoon jaunt. "Mind you're back in time to make the biscuits, girl," she called as the door closed behind Mercy.

"Yes, Granny." Mercy gave Warren an apologetic look. "You did ask to stop at home," she reminded him. "Granny does not approve of unmarried couples taking unescorted walks."

"I enjoy your brothers, and I am actually grateful for Granny's careful guardianship of you. Oscar tells me that she has discouraged more than one of your potential suitors." Warren offered his arm and smiled when she accepted it.

"If she did, I was not aware of it."

George, Knox, and Johnny led the way across a field. The stubble from last summer's hay harvest had regrown into thick clumps and layers of yellowed grasses, providing uneven footing. Mercy was obliged to accept Warren's assistance more than once when her ankles twisted slightly in hidden ruts and rabbit holes. A fox darted into the brush at their approach; Johnny's beagle set off in hot, noisy pursuit.

Warren helped Mercy over a stile, and they followed the boys into the forest. Beside the path, a swampy creek trickled between large mossy stones.

"Boys, come here."

Knox and George raced toward them. Johnny lagged behind. Tears had traced muddy paths over his round cheeks, but he struggled manfully to keep up with the older boys.

Warren firmly instructed all three boys to remain within

shouting distance, then allowed them to scamper off. Johnny paused to ask, "Are you gonna come? It's more fun when you play."

"Not this time. I must talk with your sister. Johnny, listen to me: do not take any dares. You hear?"

The little boy nodded mournfully and trotted after his brothers.

Warren found a fallen log and sat upon it, pulling Mercy down beside him. She panted lightly, looking pretty, fresh, and somewhat apprehensive. "You have played with them often lately," she stated.

Warren stretched his arms and sucked in a deep breath, then let out a long sigh. "Yes, I have. Their eldest sister seldom has time for me, so the boys have been my frequent companions."

Mercy stared at her clenched hands and chewed nervously at her lips.

After a quick glance at her troubled face, Warren suggested, "Let us take a few minutes to relax and enjoy the beauty of God's handiwork. I often find that a brief respite in the Lord's presence calms my heart and enables me to think and plan with greater clarity, viewing life's problems from a right perspective."

Taking him at his word, Mercy looked up at the canopy of trees. Dead but tenacious leaves clung to the branches of live oaks. Pines added a touch of green, and fluttering chickadees and titmice imparted life and motion to the scenery. The air was crisp with the redolence of autumn.

Warren's gaze lingered upon Mercy's face. The old bonnet had fallen back upon her shoulders. No wonder her cheeks were freckled; it seemed that she never could keep a bonnet on her head. Wisps of hair dangled about her ears and neck, loosened from her thick braided bun. There was nothing remarkable about her hair, he supposed; nonetheless, his fingers ached to touch it.

Sensing his regard, she glanced his way. "You are looking at me, not at the trees," she accused softly.

"Nevertheless, I am enjoying the beauty of God's handiwork. You are a lovely woman, Miss Jones. My eyes take pleasure in you."

Her lips tightened. His compliment did not seem to please her.

She reached down to pick up a skeleton leaf. Warren's eyes followed her every move. That shapeless dress shrouded her body, disguising its womanly shape.

"You are going away in the morning?" she asked, studying the lacy leaf as she twirled it.

"Yes, but I shall return in plenty of time for the wedding. Mercy," Warren said softly. Her questioning gaze turned to him. "These next few weeks will seem an eternity. You will not change your mind, will you? I fear my heart would break."

She shook her head. A tendril of hair curled into a loose ringlet at the soft curve where her neck connected with her shoulder. Warren lifted it in trembling fingers that barely brushed her skin.

Mercy gave a visible start and gasped.

"Pardon me! Do I frighten you, Mercy?" he asked in dismay, dropping the curl.

"In. . .in a way," she stammered. Color came and went in her smooth cheeks, and he thought she looked ready to cry.

"Does my touch disgust you?"

"No!" She covered her cheeks with trembling hands.

Gently, Warren grasped her hands and removed them from her face. Rising, he pulled her to her feet and tried to draw her closer. She resisted. "No, no!" Hearing a note of panic in her protest, he released her hands. She lost her balance, slipped on the slimy leaves, and would have fallen had Warren not caught her by the shoulders. Her hands immediately came up to push against his chest, but this time he did not let her go.

"Miss Jones, have I somehow offended you? Why have you been avoiding me?"

Her fingers grasped his lapels, and he felt the pressure of

her hands. She no longer attempted to push him away. Her eyes studied his cravat. "Granny said you would wish to spend time with Oscar and Pa, not with me."

At first he could only gape. "This is sheer folly!" The sputtering protest exploded from him. "How gained she the authority to express these. . .these hypothetical wishes? What gall! What unmitigated impudence! I traveled here to see neither your father nor even Oscar. I came to see you, my beloved Mercy."

His resentment seemed to cheer her slightly. "But I am only a woman. What can I have to say that would interest you?"

Warren's hands on her shoulders tightened. "Anything you have to say would interest me. I want to know every thought inside your lovely head. When you wrote letters to me, you shared your thoughts, your very heart. That is what I desire— to be your heart's companion. Have you forgotten everything I've told you?"

Her lower lip quivered. "Granny told me that men say pretty things when they want a woman to marry them. She said that if I desire to please you, I should stay out of your way unless you call for me. When you call for me after we are wed, I must do everything that you say, whether or not I wish to."

"What else did Granny say?" Warren inquired through tight lips. He pulled her up until she stood on tiptoe.

Hot color flooded her face. "I cannot tell you," she moaned, eyes downcast.

Fury, anxiety, and tenderness roughened his voice. "Mercy, that woman has evidently filled your head with nonsense. You need never fear me, my dearest. I would never—"

Two small boys came crashing through the bushes, laughing noisily. "Can we go back now?"

"Where is Johnny?" Warren struggled to conceal his agitation from the children.

Knox shrugged. "Back there somewhere. I'm hungry. Isn't it time for supper?"

Warren released Mercy, steadying her with one firm hand. "We will talk later," he promised, looking directly into her eyes before setting off to hunt for Johnny. He was determined to discover and allay her fears before leaving town.

But Granny Jones thwarted Warren's plans by requiring Mercy's presence for the remainder of the evening. Warren had no further opportunity to speak privately with his betrothed.

❧

"Girl, you get back in this house!" Granny thundered.

Mercy paid no heed. Barefooted, bareheaded, she dashed across the yard toward the barn, clutching a shawl at her breast. Warren was just turning his prancing horse toward the road. He waved to Oscar, Martin, and the three boys.

"Wait! Oh, wait, please!" Mercy pleaded. Would he hear her?

Buttons began to bark, dashing in circles around Mercy's flying skirts. She stumbled and nearly tripped over the silly dog. To her horror, the Colonel dropped his head between his knees and bucked. But Warren quickly controlled the horse and turned him to face her.

"Mercy!" His face brightened. "Take heed, my dear. The Colonel is very fresh."

She stopped a short distance from the skittish gelding. "I am so sorry!" she panted. "Granny forbade me to leave the house, but I had to see you. Be careful, Mr. Somerville. I will be praying for your safe return."

He was Mercy's idea of royalty in his overcoat, glossy boots, and dashing top hat. Yet his eyes glowed with love for her alone. She wanted to lift her arms and request to be taken up on his saddle again. Instead, she stood there, hopping from one cold foot to the other.

He shifted in the saddle as though he were about to dismount. Then Martin asked pointedly, "Hadn't you better be away?" Mercy's father stood with huge arms crossed over his barrel chest.

The Colonel began to prance in circles, champing at the bit until froth dripped from his mouth. Mercy saw Warren's fine lips tighten in frustration. "Write to me?" He spoke over one shoulder as the horse spun around again.

Mercy nodded. "Our mail is undependable, but I will write." Wrapping both arms around herself, she tried not to let her teeth chatter audibly.

"Better get out of this cold. Make sure you purchase a warm cape for our journey." His gentle tone felt almost as though he had caressed her cheek.

"I will."

Their eyes met for one poignant moment, then Warren gave the Colonel some rein. The horse leaped into a full gallop. When he reached the main road, Warren lifted a hand in farewell. Mercy waved back. As soon as he was out of sight, she burst into tears.

seven

A man's heart deviseth his way:
but the Lord directeth his steps.
Proverbs 16:9

Warren rapped the brass doorknocker and stepped back. A stiff breeze with a salty tang caught his hat and nearly lifted it from his head. Holding his hat in place, he spoke over his shoulder to the Colonel. "I hope someone is here."

The horse blinked and blew softly through his nose. He was exhausted both from the long journey and from the ferry rides. The Colonel held a low opinion of boats.

At last the large door opened. A tall black servant in a rich uniform regarded Warren blankly for a moment before recognition dawned in his eyes. "Mister Somerville, suh. 'Tis a pleasure to see you again."

"Hello, Horatio. It has been a long time: two years, at least, since we met in Philadelphia. Is my uncle in?"

"He and the missus are at the homestead, but I've got orders to care for you once you arrived. You come on in and make yourself to home, suh. Bonny will fix you up something fine to eat, and I'll send Leon to care for your horse." Horatio ushered Warren into the house with a wave of his arm. "Let me take those saddle bags."

Concerned and slightly embarrassed, Warren stopped in the entryway. "I don't wish to impose upon you, Horatio."

"Not at all, suh. The master will likely return before Christmas, for the missus gets lonely away from town and begs him to bring her back. We keeps ready for them always."

"Is the parsonage finished?"

Horatio beamed. "It shore is. They been hard at work, fixing

85

the place up for you. Bonny and me helped over there last week. Were you wanting to move right in tonight?"

"Perhaps I should, since Uncle Wyeth is not here. You and Bonny need your time off."

"But you'll need to eat, suh."

"I can always sneak back and beg a few scraps from Bonny. She is a kind soul." Warren lifted his rucksack to his shoulder. "Can you give me directions?"

"I can do better—I'll take you there, Mister Warren. Your trunk arrived a few weeks back; it's been awaitin' for you."

"Ah, excellent. It will be good to have fresh clothing again."

Leading the Colonel, Warren accompanied Horatio along the quiet street. A lone horseman and a few coaches rattled past. Smoke drifted from only three or four chimneys.

"You oughts to ride, suh," Horatio admonished in his kindly way.

"I've been riding these two days. I need to walk. Don't worry about this limp."

"Whatever you says."

After a short silence, Warren observed, "The town seems quiet."

"Many of the folk on this end of town are out at their plantations now that the heat and mosquitoes are gone. The sailors' families and the fishermen are still about. You'll likely have small congregations most of the winter. That's the way it is here." As they neared the eastern edge of town, Horatio stopped and pointed. A white steeple rose gracefully above bare treetops. "There she is, suh. Now ain't that a sight?"

"It is, indeed!" Warren sighed in delight. The building was classical in style, brick with white pillars framing the double doors.

"Just beyond it there, t'other side o' those trees, is the parsonage. It's almighty fine, too."

The two men circled the church building, then entered to admire its cavernous interior. Their footsteps echoed on hardwood flooring. The polished wooden pews smelled new.

Warren tried out his lectern for size and gazed up into the shadowed balcony, trying to imagine the seats filled with eager listeners. When compared to the mighty cathedrals of England the building was tiny, yet Warren thought it perfect.

While Horatio closed the front doors behind them, Warren breathed deeply of the sea air. "It is beautiful here in every way."

"They's a stable behind the parsonage. Want that I should take your horse?"

"Thank you, no. I'll care for him myself."

With Horatio's help, Warren soon had his tired horse bedded down for the night, knee deep in straw, and tucking eagerly into a manger full of sweet hay. The two men closed the stable door and headed for the house. Their shadows stretched long on the neatly trimmed grass. The house's white clapboards glowed pink beneath sunset skies.

"It is a handsome house. I had no idea the parsonage would be so large."

"Its foundation stones were ballast on one of Mr. Reynolds's ships, and much of the interior wood was imported— mahogany, teak, and pecan." Horatio sounded personally proud.

"A fine place to bring my new bride."

"Your bride?"

Warren grinned. "A Miss Mercedes Jones has consented to become my wife, and I will return to Woods Grove for her in three weeks' time."

"Do your aunt and uncle know 'bout this?" Horatio asked, looking concerned. "I have an idea that the missus wanted to find you a wife. She's been makin' plans to introduce you around."

Warren stopped on the front porch and looked thoughtfully into the other man's eyes. "Has she, indeed? I'm thankful you told me."

He opened the front door and stepped into a bright entry-way. The house had many windows; some had been left ajar to circulate fresh air. There were three rooms upstairs; down-stairs were a sitting room, hallway, and a large bedroom. The kitchen was detached to reduce the risk of fire. A porch ran across the entire front of the house, matched by a second story veranda. Many of Beaufort's houses boasted these two-story porches, Warren had observed.

He paused on the upstairs veranda, leaned on its railing, and gazed out to sea toward the barrier islands. It was a rest-ful view. Seagulls mewed along the coast. *What will she think of it? Has she ever seen the ocean?*

"You'll need to get you a housekeeper, I'm thinkin'," Horatio informed Warren. "Or ask Mr. Beauregard Reynolds to hire you out a servant. He's got a lot of people and could maybe spare one."

"I have heard of Mr. Reynolds." The thought of borrowing one of his parishioners' "people" disgusted Warren.

"He is an elder in the church, and he likes to run things."

Warren mentally stored away this information. "My uncle informed me that this church never has decided which denomination it is. Most of the members started out Anglican but have attended the Methodist and Baptist churches at vari-ous times."

"Which church do you represent, Mr. Somerville? I never have heard."

Stepping back inside, Warren answered while they descended the stairs. "Strangely enough, that question was not asked when I applied for this position. I represent the church of the Lord Jesus Christ. I was educated partly at Cambridge, partly at Princeton. I was ordained in a small chapel in New Jersey, and I care little for labels. My goal is to preach the gospel to every living creature and to encourage and equip the saints for service in this world. That is all."

He entered the master bedroom, dropped his saddlebags and rucksack on the bed, and began to unpack. A fine oak wardrobe stood against one wall, and an armoire opposite the bed. Fine furnishings for the home of a wet-behind-the-ears pastor. His relatives must have overseen these arrangements.

From the bedroom doorway behind him, Horatio warned, "Mr. Somerville, your notions may not set well with your congregation. If I was you, I'd sit quiet and listen for a spell afore I spoke my mind. I'll be praying."

"You may be right, my friend. I will appreciate your prayers."

&

Warren's first sermon as pastor of Beaufort Chapel was preached to a meager congregation consisting mainly of women, children, and the elderly. Beauregard Reynolds, a wealthy merchant, was laid up with the gout, and Captain George Nottingham, another pillar of the parish, was at sea. Other regulars, like Warren's Uncle and Aunt Wyeth, were at their plantations for the season. The gallery held black servants of assorted ages; Horatio smiled encouragingly whenever Warren looked his way.

Bolstering his sagging spirits, Warren reminded himself that each soul present was vitally important in God's sight. He proceeded to speak his message about God's grace with boldness and sincerity. "In following weeks," he announced at the close of the service, "I will be preaching a series of messages concerning prophecy leading up to Christ's birth. We will then continue on into a study of Jesus' ministry. This study should take us through Lent and Easter. I can think of no topic more interesting than the contemplation of Christ's earthly life, for He is the example of godly living which we all strive to follow."

He saw sparks of interest in a few scattered faces. One elderly man was leaning back and openly snoring—a discouraging sight for a fledgling pastor. A bearded man seated behind the sleeper tapped him firmly on the shoulder. He woke with a loud snort that caused youthful members of the congregation to sputter and choke on suppressed mirth.

Despite this disheartening episode, several people complimented Warren's sermon as he shook their hands in farewell.

One boy looked up at him with honest brown eyes and said, "I liked your talk, sir. Most things from the Bible are boring, but you made God seem interesting."

The child's horrified mother apologized and dragged him away as Warren gave him a sympathetic smile. "Listen next week; it may be even better!"

Watching from the church's front steps as carriage after carriage drove past, Warren realized that not one black man or woman had shaken his hand. Not even Horatio.

Anger tightened his lips. Despite Horatio's advice, he wanted to attack this evil system, to show these proud, stubborn Southerners the error of their ways. *How dare they treat God's children like merchandise, like animals? I would never—*

Wouldn't you? A quiet inner question interrupted his thoughts. *What about your family's hired servants? Did you treat them as your equals?*

Frowning, he considered the question. After a concerted effort, he remembered one servant's name: Leach, the butler. He had no memory of Leach's first name. Oh, yes, there also had been Rhoda, his nanny, and the private tutor Max. Rhoda had been deathly afraid of spiders; otherwise, he could recall little about her. Max had been efficient, somber, and utterly uninteresting. Warren remembered one or two other faces— the housekeeper, the groom—but even they were fuzzy. Yet many of these servants had been with the Somerville family for most of his life. They had always been there, like furniture.

During Warren's youth, the innate superiority of himself, his noble family, and his nation had been unassailable fact. Only since his commitment to follow Christ had he become aware of his arrogance.

Turning back to face the empty auditorium, Warren felt his eyes burn. He slipped into a pew and rested his forehead on his clenched hands.

Except for Your grace, I am no better than the cruelest overseer or the most heartless slave merchant that walks this earth. Had I been reared in this community, I would be as blind as these people, Your sheep. Oh, Lord, why do I still struggle with this same sin? Again and again I must recognize it in my heart, and each time I must beg Your forgiveness and mercy.

Lord, I am blind. Open my eyes; help me to see! People swarm around me every day, and seldom do I even notice them. Help me to realize that each one is precious to You. Rank, class, and color are superficial differences—before You, all are simply lost souls in need of a Savior. Break my foolish pride, Lord. Whatever it takes, please fill me with Your unselfish love! If You can use me to reach even one soul with the truth and reality of Your love, my life will not have been lived in vain.

ঌ

During the following week, Warren contacted every family presently in town. He visited Mr. Reynolds, whose gouty foot had to be elevated; he met mousy little Mrs. Reynolds and her two giggling daughters. He visited other members of the church board and was introduced to their families. He called upon the town's other ministers and established friendships with them. He could not visit the families whose husbands and fathers were at sea, however, for he did not believe it wise for a minister to visit women alone.

"Once Mercy arrives, we will call upon these ladies together," he told himself.

He spent hours walking along open beaches or riding the Colonel along the shoreline. Once, he rowed a borrowed boat to a barrier island. It was cold, windy, and desolate out there, and the Atlantic looked gray and threatening. Warren loved its majestic solitude. He carried on long conversations with God, laying out sermon plans while he walked and meditated on Scripture. He took most of his meals at a boardinghouse one block over from the church, visiting with its tenants and trying to build friendships with them.

And he dreamed of Mercy. He talked to her as he walked

along the shores, pouring out his hopes for the future, dreaming of the love they would share. The one letter he posted, however, contained merely descriptions of the parsonage, anecdotes about townsfolk, and wishes for her good health. Not only was he uncertain that she would receive it before his return, he also worried lest Granny's unfriendly eye censure any tender words he might write.

The following Sunday, a few more people occupied the wooden pews. Warren noticed several attentive faces, and Bible pages rustled when he referred to Isaiah's prophecies about the Messiah. He introduced a Christmas hymn to his flock, singing it a cappella since the church had no organ. "We will sing this each week until Christmas."

A few people joined in the second time through "Hark, the Herald Angels Sing." Warren actually spotted one or two smiles. He recognized Bonny's rich contralto from the gallery and gave her a thankful smile.

When the service ended, Warren hastened to the back and managed to greet the last few exiting slaves. They looked more shocked than pleased to shake his hand, but he felt better afterward. Horatio complimented him on the sermon, and Warren thanked Bonny for her singing. Then other church members approached, and the servants quickly disappeared.

Warren learned that the little boy who liked his sermons was Jonathan Munfrees, the son of a sailor. This week, Jonathan shook Warren's hand firmly and returned his smile.

❧

On Monday, Mercy's letter arrived.

Slipping it inside his waistcoat, Warren paid the postage and walked home, hoping no one could tell how rapidly his heart was beating. As soon as he shut the front door, he methodically removed and hung on the coat tree his hat, greatcoat, and topcoat. Loosening his cravat as he entered the sitting room, he reached for the precious letter. His fingers shook as he broke the seal and unfolded the paper.

Her handwriting looked strangely uneven and crooked.

Dear Mr. Somerville,

My father has instructed me to write this letter to you.

My grandmother's heart is paining her lately, and she vows she cannot raise this entire family without my help. Therefore my father has placed a stipulation upon his consent to our marriage.

You must agree to take and raise Johnny, my youngest brother, along with me. The older boys can be of help to my father in the smithy, but Johnny is a hindrance.

If this condition displeases you, my father offers Julianne to be your wife in my place. She is not too young to make you a good wife. Should you choose to marry Julianne, Miss Netterby has assured me that the clothing she has sewn for me could be altered to fit my sister, so your expenditures in that regard would not be wasted.

Here there was a puckered circle on the paper as though a tear had fallen. The ink in the next line was slightly smeared.

I assure you that Julianne is a lovely person in every respect. Her illness is not contagious and would not prevent her from raising a family.

I remain your willing servant,
Mercedes Jones

Warren sank upon the carved settee and rested his forehead on his open palms. The letter crackled against his ear. Almost he crumpled it and tossed it into the fireplace. Only the fact that Mercy had touched it stayed his shaking hand.

Rage mounted within him until his body could no longer contain it. His chest began to heave. Veins stood out upon his forehead and neck.

"God!" he suddenly shouted at the ceiling, shaking both clenched fists. "What is happening to me?" Rising, he kicked at the andirons, threw a pewter pitcher against the wall hard enough to leave a dent in the plaster, and slammed his fist upon a table. Heartbroken tears scalded his cheeks, but he did not know it.

"I thought she wanted to marry me! I thought this was Your perfect answer to my prayers. Why have You allowed this to happen? Her father doubtless had this trickery in mind the entire time. That grandmother has poisoned my Mercy's mind against me. And these people claim to be Christians! How can such deception be without penalty? Am I to reward their schemes? From beginning to end they desired me to take Julianne off their hands and leave them Mercy to be the surrogate mother to those children."

Warren slumped into a chair at the table and buried his face in his arms, but his thoughts raced on. He planned eloquent, scathing speeches that would express his deep contempt for a man who would place such burdens upon the shoulders of his own daughter. He even considered punching the man's stolid face—for what little good that would do. Martin Luther Jones could probably break Warren like a twig should he so choose.

At this more rational thought, a wry smile curled Warren's tight lips. Wiping his face with one hand, he flopped back in the chair. "Lord, please calm my heart and show me Your wisdom. My ravings do nothing to solve this predicament and serve only to feed bitterness in my heart. I should rejoice that he has offered me a choice instead of forbidding the marriage outright."

Rising, he paced across a fine Turkish carpet and contemplated the future. "This house has plenty of room for children. Although I had planned to fill it with our children, little Johnny is family. I can easily learn to love him. I already love him."

He fell to his knees beside the settee, bowed his head over his clenched fists, and prayed, "Lord, once again in my selfishness I fail to recall that other people besides me depend upon You for joy and provision. Perhaps You planned that Mercy and I should furnish a loving home for this child. If so, I am willing. I am your servant; use me as You will."

Deep in prayer, Warren noticed nothing until he heard a knock at the sitting room door. "Mistah Warren?"

Starting upright, he ran a hand back through his wild hair. "Hello, is that you, Bonny?"

The door opened, revealing Bonny's anxious face. "I hope I don't be intrudin', Mistah Warren. I brung you supper. Me and Horatio thought mebbe you could use a good square meal. I doan think you been eatin' right. I knocked at the door, but you din answer."

Warren scrambled to his feet, eager to reassure the good-hearted woman. "I lack sufficient words to express how delightful one of your suppers sounds, Bonny. Did you bring some of your hush puppies?"

"You just bet I did!" Bonny smiled in relief. "And fried sole, greens, and grits. We been worried about you, Preacher. You're needin' someone to take care of you, that's sure." Her sharp eyes had not missed his disheveled appearance.

Warren folded down his collar and tried again to smooth his hair. "I could not agree more. In fact, I will be leaving town early tomorrow morning. I plan to return by Sunday. I will bring my wife and her young brother with me when I return."

"Your wife? Horatio told me you was thinkin' on marriage. That's right fine, Mistah Warren. If any man was needin' a wife, it's you."

"My sentiments exactly. I must inform the board members of my impending absence. Oh, I just recalled that there is a board meeting Saturday night. I must return in time to attend."

While eating, Warren planned his journey. As soon as he had cleared his plate and thanked Bonny, he rushed to his room to pack.

Bonny cleared up after him, shaking her turbaned head over his distracted air. "That boy do need a good woman, Lord," she prayed aloud. "I just hope to goodness You've showed him the right one."

❧

At last the familiar housetops of Woods Grove appeared over a low ridge. Although Warren wanted to gallop to town, he took pity on his exhausted horse and left him at a walk. "My legs are tired too, Colonel. Soon we'll have our rest."

Instead of rushing immediately to the Jones homestead, he stopped at Wentworth's General Store. The Colonel was no longer steaming, so Warren left his horse at the rail while he scouted out the territory. Letty might be able to give him vital information about Mercy's situation.

He scraped his boots, stepped through the door, and nearly bumped into Mercy Jones. Her eyes were red-rimmed and moist. "Oh! Warren!" Both hands lifted to cover her mouth.

Warmth filled his heart at the first sound of his given name upon her lips. His arms lifted—then abruptly fell when he noticed other people crowded into the store. Beside the stove sat the ever-present checker players, intent upon yet another game. Letty Wentworth was cutting cloth for a customer. In the far corner, Julianne Jones stood upon a stool with her arms outstretched while a woman pinned the hem of her flowing ivory gown. Granny Jones perched regally upon a nearby chair and directed the procedure.

"Mr. Somerville," Mercy's hands fluttered anxiously. "I cannot tell you how pleased I am to see you." She reached out to touch his arm as though to assure herself that he was real. "Granny, look who has come!"

Eliza Jones glanced their way and stiffened. His arrival certainly did not give her pleasure.

Suspicion filled Warren's heart. While Mercy still wore her old brown dress, the garment Julianne was having fitted looked very much like a bridal gown. The pretty blonde girl appeared miserable. A coughing fit suddenly seized her, and she wheezed as though each breath would be her last. Warren fleetingly wondered if Julianne had done it to discourage his interest.

Granny, who appeared remarkably hearty for an invalid,

recovered from her initial shock. "So you've come back early, have you? I suppose you received Mercy's letter."

"I did. I was grieved to learn that you are in ill health, madam. Since the large wedding party you had originally planned must now be impossible, I have decided that Mercy and I should simply have a small family ceremony immediately. Reverend Snowdon will be amenable, I am confident, once I explain my time limitations."

A murmur of startled gasps and exclamations followed this pronouncement. Gathering her scattered wits, Granny swept across the room, grabbed Warren's arm, and snapped, "Come with me. We must discuss this in private, Mr. Somerville. You appear to be laboring under a misapprehension."

Strong woman though she was, her grasp left him unmoved. "If that is so, I beg you to enlighten me here and now."

Cold blue eyes impaled him. "I do not discuss family matters in a public forum, sir. If you intend to take my granddaughter to wife, you will heed my bidding," she hissed.

He relented. "Very well. I require Mercy to attend our discussion, however, since it concerns her future as well as mine."

Granny hurriedly donned her shawl and bonnet. "You keep working on that dress, Miss Netterby," she instructed firmly. "I shall return."

Warren took Mercy's hand and wrapped it around his arm, then followed Granny through the door. Granny did not wait for him to untie the Colonel. She marched, head high and back straight, toward the Jones cabin.

Warren was in no hurry. He tried to hide his limp, but the weak leg gave him uncertain support. His horse bunted him in the back as they strolled along the muddy, rutted street. "I know, my good fellow. Soon you'll be in a comfortable stall."

"He looks tired," Mercy observed quietly. "So do you."

"He and I have good reason. But why do you look so wan and thin, my dear?"

"You read my letter. Granny is certain you will choose to marry Julianne rather than be saddled with Johnny. I do not wish to believe ill of my loved ones, but I fear they planned it this way almost from the start."

"Your suspicions confirm my own. Mercy, as far as I am concerned, this changes nothing. We shall take Johnny and raise him along with our own children. If this is God's will for us, I shall not object. I would also be willing, at some future date, to welcome your sister as our houseguest for an extended period. The sea air may be beneficial to her health, and I imagine you would enjoy her companionship. Once we are married, your family becomes my family, and I will gladly shoulder every responsibility thereby entailed. However, I do not intend to allow your father and grandmother additional time to think of deterrents to our marriage. We will marry tomorrow and set out for Beaufort forthwith."

Her grasp on his arm tightened. Tears streamed down her cheeks. Was she happy? He could only hope so.

eight

Let each one of you in particular so love his wife even as himself; and the wife see that she reverence her husband.
Ephesians 5:33

"Oh, Mercy, I am so thankful Mr. Somerville arrived before Miss Lucy could alter your beautiful gown. It did not look half so fine on me, I know." Julianne finished buttoning Mercy's dress up the back as she spoke.

Mercy smiled wistfully over her shoulder. "I am thankful, too Julianne, I am terribly sorry for the hateful things I thought about you these last few days! I know you never wanted to steal him away, but the idea of it hurt me so, and I had wicked thoughts."

Julianne looked up, her blue eyes misty. "I knew you must be hating me, and it seemed that I would shrivel away inside. We should have trusted God more, the both of us. And you should have trusted your Mr. Somerville, Mercy. He loves you very much. I can tell."

"Yes, but what does love mean to a man?" Mercy sighed. She slid both palms down over her hips, enjoying the silken texture of her gown. "Granny has warned me not to expect more from him than he can give. A man seeks a wife in order to gratify his own needs and desires. Mr. Somerville admits that he needs me, but I wonder at times if he realizes that I, too, have needs."

"I'm sure he must know, Mercy. He is a minister, after all."

"But Reverend Snowdon is a minister, and look at his wife. She is a miserable little creature, a mouse. I hope my husband does not expect me to be a mouse. I will do my best to be a submissive wife, though I fear that my temperament will interfere with my good intentions."

"Your hands are shaking, Mercy. Why are you nervous?

You have loved Mr. Somerville for years, and now you are to marry him. How pleased Calvin would be!"

A fleeting smile touched Mercy's face. "I wish he could be here. If I am nervous, it is only because. . ."

"Because?" Julianne prompted when her sister's voice trailed away.

"Because I do not know what Mr. Somerville will expect of me. I mean, when we are alone. Granny has told me about marital relations."

"And?" Julianne sounded breathless.

Mercy chewed her lip, looking uncertain. "I do not think I should discuss it with you. Granny says that children make a woman's lot bearable, but she looked mournful when she said it."

Julianne waved a hand in dismissal. "You know Granny. She has always been a pessimist. Do you not find Mr. Somerville attractive?"

Mercy swallowed hard. "It frightens me how I feel when he is near. I admire the way he looks and speaks and moves, and I want to touch him and be near him. But whenever I reveal these feelings, he seems uneasy, almost alarmed. I asked Granny if my feelings were normal, and she said that the Bible tells us to flee youthful lusts. She said that a minister like Mr. Somerville should not have a wife who allows such thoughts to enter her mind. I have prayed for God to remove these sinful feelings, and yet they persist. I fear that I will not be able to hide them from my husband. And yet, what can I do? Is this part of God's curse upon women, how He told Eve that she would desire her husband but he would rule over her? I am confused and frightened, Julianne—and yet, the thought of losing Mr. Somerville forever frightens me still more! What can I do?"

"Oh, my dear—"

A knock at the door startled both girls. Mercy sucked in a quick sob.

"The minister has arrived. Ready, Mercedes?" Although Martin Jones sounded gruff, he had resigned himself to the marriage. Mercy was grateful. Her grandmother had taken to her bed and refused even to attend the small ceremony.

"I am nearly ready, Pa," she called softly. "Hurry, Julianne, my cap."

Julianne settled the delicate lace cap upon her sister's hair and pinned it. "Now it should stay in place through a tempest."

"Let us hope it won't need to," Mercy said seriously. "Is every button fastened?"

Julianne inspected her sister from lace cap to satin slippers. The gown of ivory satin flowed over Mercy's figure, its Grecian lines emphasizing her graceful height. The wide neckline revealed her sloping shoulders and firm throat, and a fitted bodice outlined her womanly curves. Its cut was more daring than Mercy would have chosen without Letty's prompting. Her clean, smoothly coiled hair gleamed. The freckles sprinkled across her pert nose seemed to accentuate the purity of her skin.

"You're beautiful, Mercy. What a difference clothing makes!"

"You are lovely, too, Julianne."

"I wish Ma could be here."

Mercy nodded. "I do, too. Yet I feel that she must know. God would not keep such news secret." Just as her sister reached for the door, she grasped Julianne's hand. "Pray for me?"

"Of course I shall, you goose. Now make haste, or Mr. Somerville will fear that you have climbed out a window and run away."

Though morning light filtered through a few small windows, it could not reach the cabin's dark corners. Martin had lighted a few lamps and set them about the room, and a huge fire blazed upon the hearth. Rev. Snowdon spoke quietly with Warren at one end of the room while George, Knox, and Johnny wrestled and giggled at the other end. Helen, wearing a made-over gown of Julianne's, looked up from her book as the older girls entered. Letty Wentworth stood beside her father near the door, looking uncomfortable. Her face brightened when Mercy smiled.

Martin sprawled in his chair before the fire. Mercy knew her father was nervous, for smoke puffs rose from his pipe at a faster rate than normal. He glanced up at Mercy and started in surprise. Quickly covering his reaction, he growled, "You look well, my dear."

"Thank you, Pa." Mercy's heart warmed. His eyes had revealed affection and sorrow.

She glanced up at Warren and felt a shock down to her toes. He was always handsome, but today his physical perfection electrified her. His cropped brown curls were in unusually good order. A pristine white shirtfront, cravat, and waistcoat contrasted perfectly with his black cutaway coat and breeches. Usually, she had noticed, his gray eyes remained nearly hidden behind their screen of lashes. Just now, however, she could see them from across the room, for they had widened appreciatively at the sight of her.

Her entire body trembled in reaction. *How will I ever survive this day?*

In a daze, she accepted her father's arm, took her place before the minister, and listened to the opening words of his short message. When her father released her to Warren's care, her heart felt too large for her body, as though it had no room in which to beat. She spoke her vows sedately and allowed Warren to slip a gold ring upon her finger. The minister declared them man and wife according to the laws of North Carolina. She and Warren signed the license, then Letty and her father signed as witnesses.

Hugs and kisses from Julianne and Helen. A hug and tears from her father. Letty exclaimed over her beauty and explained in detail something about a bonnet. Mercy smiled and nodded as though she understood. George and Knox hugged her so tightly that she could scarcely draw breath. Johnny was crying, clinging to his father's leg. His dog, Buttons, sat at his feet. Granny emerged from her room long enough to gift Mercy with a small leather pouch. Teary eyed, she kissed the girl roughly on the cheek and told her to get on. In a blur, Mercy gathered up her few scattered things and watched the men load satchels and baskets into the coach's boot. Oscar placed the step at the carriage door, and Mercy climbed into the coach's musty interior.

"May we have a word of prayer before beginning our journey?" Warren suggested. He stood just outside the carriage door with one booted foot on the step. Removing his hat, he bowed his head and waited for silence. The Jones family grew quiet. Mercy bowed her head but peered out the open window at her family. In the gray morning light, they appeared rather shabby and sad. Martin's huge shoulders slumped. A knot formed in Mercy's stomach, and her tears overflowed, leaving damp circles where they fell upon her lustrous skirts.

"Lord, we ask your blessing on this family. Please grant them strength, joy, and mercy to replace the Oscar, Johnny, and Mercy they have given into my care. Fill them with Your love and provide for their every need in accordance with their dependence upon You. I request also Your blessing upon my new family and upon our journey. Keep the four of us safe and well, and guide us into Your paths in all that we do and say. We desire to be light and salt to everyone we meet in our travels. Please fill us with Your unselfish love, and open our eyes to the needs of others. I make these requests in Jesus' name."

Warren's earnest prayer soothed Mercy's spirit. Her sorrow eased as she remembered that God cared more about her family than she did. With every throb of her heart she echoed Warren's blessing.

Martin lifted Johnny into the carriage. The little boy flung himself upon Mercy and clung to her, crying quietly. The beagle hopped up after him and settled at his feet. Her ears were flattened, her tail tucked. Enormous brown eyes begged for acceptance.

Warren paused with one foot on the step. His eyes slowly lifted to meet Mercy's startled gaze. The dog had never been mentioned as part of this deal. Then Warren stepped into the coach and sat in the opposite seat. His left leg extended stiffly across the space between seats. Buttons shifted to make room for his foot, sighed, and settled with her chin on his ankle.

Glancing pointedly at the dog, Mercy mouthed a "Thank you" to her husband.

He only smiled.

Martin reached through the open door to shake his son-in-law's hand. "Take good care of them," he ordered gruffly before closing the door.

Warren nodded. "With all my heart."

Martin bellowed an order. The carriage lurched.

They were off.

ঽ

At noon, they stopped near a beaver pond and climbed out to stretch their legs. Oscar watered the team; Warren untied the Colonel from the back of the coach and led him down the bank for a drink. Buttons went wild with happiness, baying at a rabbit and bounding through the brush. Mercy and Johnny stepped into the woods to take care of private business. When they returned, Oscar and Warren took their turn, disappearing into the cold, swampy forest. Looking about at the tangle of wilderness, Mercy shuddered. She did not relax until Warren reappeared. He was limping again. The carriage ride must have stiffened his leg.

"Hungry? Your family packed a basket luncheon," Warren announced, lifting it from the boot. "There is plenty for all of us and to spare."

They stood near the coach and perched on its step, munching on cold roast beef, baked potatoes, bread, and apples. A swig from Warren's water skin washed the meal down. Buttons accepted all donations, intentional or accidental. Her white-tipped tail wagged ceaselessly. The horses ate grain from their nosebags, muscles bunching in their big jaws as they noisily chewed.

The sun made a tentative attempt to break through and offer warmth. Mercy lifted her face to its feeble rays and closed her eyes, clutching her new cloak around her shoulders.

"I've been meaning to congratulate you, Lefty," Oscar commented into the long silence. "You got yourself one fine wife."

Mercy returned Oscar's wide smile as Warren said, "Thank

you. I did, indeed. And a fine brother into the bargain." He squeezed Johnny's thin shoulders.

"And a dog." The little boy leaned into Warren and sighed deeply. "Why does Oscar call you 'Lefty,' Mr. Somerville?"

"Your brother Calvin first addressed me by that disrespectful title," Warren frowned.

Grinning, Oscar finished the explanation. "If you had heard this fellow introduce himself as 'Leftenant Summahville' in that high-and-mighty way of his, you'd understand why. He'll always be Lefty to me."

"I thought I had forever left that appellation behind me," Warren sighed. "Now it follows me where'er I go."

"Can I call you Lefty?" Johnny's blond locks stood on end as he peered up at Warren's face.

"You may. I suppose it will not kill me." Warren hoisted the boy upon his shoulders. Johnny shifted Warren's hat to his own head and whooped. His shouts echoed through the surrounding trees. Buttons leaped about them, ears flapping, baying in one continuous howl. Warren dumped Johnny to the ground and snatched for his hat, but Johnny dodged and ran, laughing. Warren limp-hopped after him, grabbing at and missing the boy's dangling shirttail. Oscar leaned against the coach door and made disparaging remarks about his friend's reflexes and advanced age.

Mercy smiled as she watched them. Her husband looked relaxed and happy. Before leaving her father's house, he had changed into riding clothes: a dark green wool topcoat over a silvery print waistcoat and tan breeches. Mercy wished she had changed, too. Her wedding gown offered little warmth.

By the time everyone climbed aboard the carriage, the horses were well rested and Johnny was exhausted. His round cheeks were flushed. This time he took the seat beside Warren. Buttons resumed her former position, emitting a resigned sigh before resting her head on Warren's polished boot. Mercy caught Warren smiling at her when she looked up from the beagle.

❧

Blinking, Mercy sat up and realized that she must have been napping. The coach was slowing. Across from her, Johnny sat up and yawned. "Are we almost there?"

"No, we are there," Warren said calmly. "Did you rest well, Mrs. Somerville?"

The title startled Mercy. "Yes. Yes, I think I did. How long was I asleep?"

"I cannot say, for I have been awake no more than half an hour. When I rode through town the other day, I reserved a room for us at this inn."

Peering through the side window, Mercy realized that the coach had stopped before a brick building. The door suddenly opened, and Oscar placed a step for her.

"Thank you, Oscar." Taking his hand, she stepped carefully down.

"You two go on inside. You should have time to wash before dinner. I shall join you after Oscar and the horses are settled." Warren returned to help unload bags.

Johnny skipped up the steps beside Mercy. "What are you waiting for?" he demanded. "It's cold out here."

Mercy followed her little brother inside.

"Mrs. Somerville?" A plump, smiling man approached them. "I am Amos Pritchard. We have been expecting your arrival. Come right this way. And may I offer my felicitations upon your recent marriage?"

Mercy smiled and thanked her host, waiting while he instructed his servants to hurry and bring in the guests' luggage. "We have provided a roll-away bed for the child; I hope this will be adequate."

"I am certain that it will," Mercy agreed faintly. This was her first experience with an inn. She had no idea what to expect or demand. Johnny gripped her hand and followed her upstairs with Buttons at his heel. Apparently, the innkeeper did not object to dogs, for he made no comment.

The room seemed immense to Mercy and Johnny. An

enormous canopied bed dominated the space. Mahogany side tables and velvet draperies gleamed in the light of Mr. Pritchard's candle. The proprietor quickly lit the oil lamps as two black men entered, carrying luggage. He directed them where to place it. "Madam, should you need anything, pull that cord," he directed, "and my servants will assist you. We dine at eight. Tonight's menu is venison roast with chestnut stuffing."

Mercy smiled acknowledgment and closed the door behind him. Her eyes returned to that prodigious bed. Slowly, she removed her bonnet and hung it on a wall hook.

Johnny immediately jumped upon the feather tick that lay at the bed's foot. "This one is mine. I'm tired, Mercy. When can we go to bed?"

"Not until after supper," she informed him. "We must wash and change before then."

"You wash. I want to sleep."

Mercy refrained from comment, although this was the first time in her memory that such words had escaped the child's lips. Slipping behind a wooden screen, she began to unbutton her travel-wilted gown. It was difficult to reach the buttons in the middle of her back, but she managed. Having nowhere else to place the gown, she shook it out and draped it over the screen. After pouring fresh water into the china basin, she splashed her face and arms, trying to keep her chemise dry.

The chamber door opened and footsteps creaked on the wooden floorboards. "Johnny? Why are you in bed? It is not yet time to retire," Warren said softly, closing the door. Mercy heard the rustle as he removed and hung up several garments.

She froze, hands clasped under her chin. Gooseflesh rose on her bare arms and shoulders. The satchel containing her gowns still waited beside the bed. She had no choice but to put on her wedding dress again unless she wished to appear before her husband in petticoats, chemise, and corset.

Johnny sounded grumpy. "I'm waiting my turn to wash. Mercy takes too long. When do we get to eat?"

"Soon. How did Buttons get in here?"

"She followed us. Don't send her away!"

"We shall be obliged to take her outside before we retire, Johnny. I suppose we can bring her scraps to eat. I am surprised that Pritchard allowed a dog upstairs."

Mercy peered over the top of the screen. Mr. Somerville's back was to her. His shirt was untucked, and he was loosening his cravat. His unfolded shirt collar rose above his earlobes. "You'd better change into a clean shirt for dinner, John."

"I haven't got one."

"Then we must make do with that one until we can purchase another." Warren dropped the wilted cravat over a chair and unbuttoned his shirt. Mercy watched in fascination. When he turned toward her, she ducked.

"Mercy?" he spoke quietly from the other side of the screen, only inches away. "Are you nearly finished?"

"Just a moment." Her hands shook and her heart pounded as she pulled the gown back over her head and let its rich folds settle over her petticoats. The buttons were harder to fasten than they had been to unfasten. She tucked a few loose hairs into place, pinched her cheeks, and stepped from behind the screen.

Warren perched on the side of the bed, clad in breeches, boots, and an unbuttoned shirt. Mercy felt her cheeks grow hot, but she tried to appear calm.

"Leave any water for the rest of us?" Warren smiled and rose. "You look beautiful, my dear."

She said only "Thank you" and sidled past him without breathing, headed toward Johnny's baggage. The boy did have another shirt, for she had sewn it herself the week before. Concentrating on her little brother helped return her heart rate to normal. Johnny fussed and complained as usual, attempting to evade her efforts to tuck in his fresh shirt.

"Let me help," Warren ordered from behind her. He quickly had the boy's face washed, his hair smoothed, and his shirt tucked in neatly.

Mercy was relieved to see that her husband was now fully clothed. His slicked back hair was already escaping into curls.

Granny had declared curly hair inappropriate for a minister. The memory made Mercy's lips twitch, and yet she could not help thinking that it did seem improper, even unfair, for a man of God to be so handsome.

"Let us make one point perfectly clear from the beginning, John Wesley Jones," he was saying soberly. "Your sister and I are in charge of your discipline as well as your care. You will obey her commands and mine as you would obey your father's, or I will make your life difficult. Do you understand me?"

Wide-eyed, Johnny nodded. His lower lip trembled.

Softening, Warren gave the boy a hug. "I am glad to have you with us, Johnny. We will have a good life together."

Mercy's heart swelled with admiration and affection. As Warren rose and donned his topcoat, he suddenly looked up, catching her gaze. Turning away, she nervously lifted a hand to smooth her hair.

"Wait," he said quietly. "Your buttons are not lined up."

"Oh!" She reached a hand back. Her face burned. "I was too hasty."

He rectified her mistake without actually touching her back. Mercy keenly felt his presence, his hands and warm breath. She kept recalling that glimpse of his lean body. "Finished." He touched her shoulders, and she started as though he had shocked her. His hands quickly fell away, and he stepped back.

"Are we ready? It is time to go down."

"I'm starved," Johnny announced, heading for the door. Warren offered Mercy his arm, and she accepted shyly. She felt ridiculous beyond words for her overreaction to his touch. What must he think?

Holding back for a moment, Warren murmured into Mercy's ear. "I wish to apologize for embarrassing you. I am unaccustomed to sharing quarters, and I did not reflect on your feelings before disrobing. I shall try to be more considerate in the future."

Her face burning, Mercy could only nod.

nine

*My son, despise not the chastening of the Lord; neither
be weary of his correction: for whom the Lord loveth he
correcteth; even as a father the son in whom he delighteth.*
Proverbs 3:11-12

Mercy stirred and lifted a hand to brush hair from her face. A
knee jabbed into her back. Rolling over, she prepared to
shove her sister away, then noticed that she was not lying
upon the loft floor. Instead of her cornshuck bolster, a soft
feather tick shifted and billowed beneath her. Heavy curtains
hung around the bed.

All at once, memories of the wedding and the journey
flooded her mind. After their quiet supper, Warren had gone
out to check on Oscar, leaving Johnny and Mercy to themselves. *I fell asleep. I thought I would lie awake until he came
in, yet I never heard him come to bed. He is here beside me!*
The thought sent blood surging to her face and set every
nerve a-tingle. Deep breathing told her that he slept, so she
reached out a tentative hand.

The hair beneath his nightcap felt silky instead of curly.
Her fingers moved to his face and felt smooth skin. A nightshirt draped over slender shoulders. Johnny?

Disappointment nearly crushed her. Although she had been
terrified to spend the night with her husband, her fear was
strangely blended with anticipation. Had he not come to bed
at all? A longing for Warren overcame her fears.

Mercy sat up. The room was very cold, she discovered as
soon as the quilt fell from her shoulders. Her new cambric
nightgown could not keep out the piercing chill. Something
warm upon her feet turned out to be Buttons, snoring softly in

her sleep. *My wedding night, shared with my baby brother and a dog. But who pulled the bed curtains?*

Mercy had never before slept in a canopied bed. It was very dark within those curtains. Without forethought, she reached across Johnny and checked to make sure Warren had not come to bed. She checked too vigorously. Her open palm connected solidly with a body. "Unh!" grunted a deep voice as a hand gripped her arm.

Mercy squealed.

"Hush," Warren said calmly.

Johnny muttered in his sleep, then settled again.

"Oh!" she gasped more quietly. "You are here! I never heard you come. I am sorry for clouting you."

His whisper sounded amused. "Now that you know I am here, may I sleep?"

Her teeth began to chatter. "Yes, of course."

"You are cold. Our fire had expired before I returned to the room. Johnny probably joined us in bed because he was cold, poor lad. Here." He released Mercy's hand. She heard and felt him moving about in the bed; then Johnny was no longer beside her.

"What are you doing?" she whispered. Somehow she felt bolder in the darkness.

"Shifting Johnny to my other side. I'll wrap an arm around each of you, and we will all be warmer. Come, lie down, and I'll cover you with the quilt."

Hesitantly, Mercy lay down beside her husband, then scooted closer and rested her cheek upon his shoulder. His arm came around her, pulling her close. Her hand rested on his chest; she felt and heard the strong beat of his heart. His nightshirt was soft to her touch. At first she was intensely aware of his warm body against hers. Could he feel her trembling? But when he lay perfectly still, she gradually relaxed against him—even snuggled a little closer. For a moment he stopped breathing, then released the breath in a tremulous sigh.

Just before sleep claimed her, she felt Warren kiss the top

of her head. "I love you, Mercy." The whisper barely reached her ears.

❧

When Mercy awakened the next morning, only Johnny slept beside her in the big bed. There was a deep depression in the tick where Warren had lain; she nestled into it with a sigh, recalling the warmth and tenderness of his embrace. *Granny was mistaken,* she realized. *I believe I shall enjoy being Mr. Somerville's wife.*

Something stirred inside the bedchamber. Mercy crawled to the corner of the bed and pushed aside a curtain. Warren was adding wood to the stove, blowing into a small fire. He was already dressed for the day, though his hair looked wild. As she watched, he settled into a chair and opened his Bible to a marked page, reading by candlelight.

Mercy settled back into the bed and stared up at the high canopy. *Dear God, thank You for leading me to marry Mr. Somerville. Please show me how to be the wife he needs. I want very much to please him, but I truly do not know how. If I read the Bible more, would it teach me to be a good wife like Mama was? I want to know You better, and I want to love You the way Calvin and Mama did—the way Mr. Somerville and Oscar do.*

She dozed off in the midst of her prayer.

"Time to begin the day, sluggards."

The cheerful order penetrated Mercy's dreams like a dash of cold water.

Warren hauled back the bedcurtains. "I am going to help Oscar with the horses and coach. I will take Buttons with me. Prepare to break your fast in thirty minutes. We must not tarry today."

Blinking as though the gray light of dawn hurt her eyes, Mercy sat up and yawned. "I'm coming." She pulled off her nightcap and began unbraiding her hair.

Johnny never moved. Warren reached over and jiggled the boy. "John, I keep a water pitcher handy for use on lazy boys. Come now."

Mercy heard the iron undertone in that pleasant voice. She was not surprised when Johnny rubbed his eyes with both fists and sat up.

Fresh bread, cheese, and grapes filled their bellies before their journey resumed. Since the other guests had not yet come downstairs, the travelers had the dining room to themselves.

"Has Oscar eaten?"

"Yes, I took him food earlier," Warren replied, then popped a grape into his mouth. "The horses are hitched and ready. Make haste, please."

Mercy felt he was being unreasonable. "Why the hurry and flurry?"

"I have business in town and people to see upon our return. I must arrive home expeditiously. I am sorry to impel you, but it must be so."

Mercy frowned. On her wedding trip she must hurry because her new husband was concerned about business? "I wish to return to our room before we leave. I require something from my satchel."

"I am afraid our baggage has already been taken to the coach. You gave me to understand that you were prepared to leave."

Mercy detected a slight edge to his voice, but she persisted. "I forgot this item."

A muscle twitched in his jaw. "Tell me which bag, and I will fetch it for you."

"The one with a black handle."

"If you are finished. . ."

Mercy rose from the table and took hold of Johnny's hand. She found Warren's attitude irritating. He was being unpleasant about the matter.

The horses stamped impatiently while the satchel was unearthed from the boot and Mercy removed from it one cambric hankie. She caught Warren and Oscar exchanging a glance, and her cheeks warmed. Lifting the skirts of her new traveling suit, she allowed Warren to assist her into the coach.

Johnny settled beside her, and the dog sat at his feet.

"I shall ride up top with Oscar for a while," Warren informed them through the window. "You will have more room that way."

Mercy nodded, once again too surprised to react. Johnny immediately leaped to the opposite seat and lay down, kicking up his heels. "C'mon, Buttons. We can play now!"

The coach lurched into motion; buildings began to rush past the windows on either side. Soon trees replaced the buildings. The coach swayed from side to side and bounced over ruts in the road.

During the first long hours of travel, Mercy stared through the window to her left and fought back tears. Had she angered her husband with her demand for a clean handkerchief? Was he already weary of her company?

"Mercy, I'm all bloody!" Johnny exclaimed suddenly.

Mercy gasped. Blood dripped from the boy's nose, covered his hands, and soaked into his shirtfront and cuffs. He had already smeared it up to his forehead.

Instantly, the handkerchief came into use. Pressing it to his face, she bade him lie down. He coughed and protested, but eventually obeyed. Kneeling before his seat, Mercy forgot about possible blood on the floorboards. Once the bleeding had stopped and she returned to her seat, she saw that the front of her skirt was spotted and smeared.

"Oh no!" she wailed. "My new suit!"

Rising, she knocked on the coach's ceiling, trying to gain her husband's attention. The men must have been deep in conversation, for they did not seem to notice her efforts. She tugged and pulled at the side window, but could not decipher its release mechanism. Feeling somewhat claustrophobic, she pounded on the ceiling with her fists and shouted. Johnny joined in, and Buttons began to howl and bark.

Suddenly, a rectangular panel above Johnny's seat slid open and Warren peered in at them. "Are you calling us?"

"Yes!" Mercy shouted. "Stop, please!"

The coach slowed to a halt, and Warren flung open the door. "Are you ill?"

"We've been pounding and calling for ever so long. Why did you not stop?"

Surprised by Mercy's vehemence, he said only, "Why did you not use the communication door?" He pointed to the small panel. "I made use of it earlier today. Surely you observed it."

Embarrassed by her lack of attention, Mercy said nothing. Her sole consolation was that Johnny had not remembered it either.

Then Warren took a good look at Johnny. "Whatever happened? Is he injured?"

"His nose bled. Although he has a tendency to nosebleeds, I have never before seen one like this. Please, are we near a stream or river where we could wash?"

Warren turned his head, considering the road ahead. "A drive of perhaps ten minutes will bring us to another bend in the Neuse River. You might use water from our bag if you cannot wait longer."

"We will wait. I am thankful that I had a handkerchief with me." Mercy could not resist adding that remark.

Warren only glanced at her, then closed the coach door and climbed back up to the seat. The coach listed under his weight until he settled into place.

"Are you and Mr. Somerville angry at each other?" Johnny asked.

"I am not angry at Mr. Somerville, but I fear that he is angry with me."

"I'm glad he's not angry at me. He kind of scares me when he's angry."

"Are you afraid that he would harm you?" Mercy's brows knitted.

"Naw. I like him a lot. He says he loves me, Mercy."

Considering these apparently conflicting statements, Mercy only nodded.

When the coach stopped again, she gathered her skirts and

climbed out after Johnny. Warren regarded the stains on her suit. "What a shame. It is a pretty dress. Do you require assistance?"

Mercy's heart skipped a beat at the compliment, but pride demanded that she hide her feelings.

"I believe we can manage. I regret the further delay." She did not sound particularly sorry.

"It cannot be helped. A stream crosses the road ahead just before joining with the Neuse. The water should be clean enough. If you are certain you do not require my aid, I will water the Colonel. The coach horses will drink when we cross."

"I am certain."

The stream flowed among many round, smooth stones. Its banks were steep, so Mercy balanced midstream upon a large rock. She squatted down to rinse out the handkerchief and dab at her skirt. The cold water immediately faded the stains.

Warren led his horse to the water downstream. Without comment, he watched Mercy while the Colonel drank. Feeling self-conscious, she tried to make her every movement graceful and sure.

Once the handkerchief was clean, she extended it to Johnny and bade him use it to wipe his face. Busy searching for minnows, he ignored her.

"Johnny, listen. Mr. Somerville is in a hurry. Take the handkerchief and use it, or I will scrub you myself."

"I already washed my hands and face. See?" The boy impatiently showed her his hands, which were clean up to the wrists. A few pale streaks crisscrossed the brown stains on his chubby face.

"Not well enough. Come stand on this stone, love, and I will wash you. Have a care; don't fall in. The stones are not slippery; you should be fine." She extended a hand to him, but he pulled back.

"I'm clean already. Leave me alone!" He slapped at her hand.

Outraged, Mercy jerked upright, lost her balance, and

stepped back with one foot. Icy water filled her slipper and dragged at her skirt. Arms flailing, she struggled to remain upright, took several plunging steps backward, and sat down hard on the opposite bank. Leafless brambles snagged her jacket and bonnet. Her first thought was abject relief that she had not sat down in the water. Her second thought was an unbounded desire for revenge.

Johnny burst into giggles. Reading his sister's expression, he suddenly turned and dashed back toward the coach. A strong hand arrested his flight.

"Do you recall my warning from yesterday? You will obey your sister, or you will answer to me, John Wesley Jones."

Johnny looked up into Warren's eyes and quailed. "I'm sorry!" he squeaked.

In reply, Warren hauled the already howling boy into the thick brush. While Mercy extricated herself from blackberry brambles and wrung out her skirts, she listened for evidence of due retribution.

The Colonel grazed quietly on long grass beside the stream. He lifted his head when Mercy slogged ashore. "At what are you staring?" she growled. The horse shook his mane and blew softly through his nostrils. He approached Mercy and bunted her gently, requesting attention. "At least you do not mock my clumsiness," she sighed, stroking his blazed face.

Holding his lead rope, she headed back to the coach, her slippers making squishy sounds with each step. Oscar took the rope from her, studied her sodden skirt, and said not one word. Her expression undoubtedly discouraged comment.

Moments later, Johnny emerged from the forest, suddenly quite willing to have his face and hands thoroughly scrubbed. His eyes were red from crying, but he looked at Mercy with new respect. An awesome force now backed her authority.

She made quick work of the mop-up job and ushered her brother back into the coach. Her husband held her hand as she climbed up; he did not release his grip after she was seated.

"Will you be all right, or would you like me to ride inside with you?"

Though she almost recommended that he do as he pleased, a sudden attack of honesty made her beg, "Would you please stay?" Shamefaced, she lifted pleading eyes to his face.

He dropped her hand and stepped back. Her heart sank until she heard him call, "Oscar, I shall ride inside. You know the turn for New Bern?"

"I do. If you like, Johnny may ride up here with me."

Johnny was thrilled with this idea. Warren glanced at Mercy, then nodded assent. They both desired privacy. Johnny scrambled up beside Oscar, already talking at full speed.

Warren stowed the step, climbed into the coach, and settled across from Mercy. His expression was cheerful. "You had better remove your shoes, my dear." He took her feet into his lap, pulled off her wet slippers and stockings, and began to rub with his strong fingers. Mercy stared at him, her lips parted in surprise.

"Does it help?"

She nodded. Her feet looked white in his brown hands. Delicious thrills ran up her legs with each gentle stroke of his fingers. His eyes held hers, promising pleasures to come. Mercy swallowed hard.

"How. . .how much farther?"

"Another three or four hours yet," Warren said apologetically.

Struggling to sound normal, Mercy blurted, "Thank you for your help with Johnny, Mr. Somerville. None of my brothers consider me an authority figure; I am only a bossy sister to them. I believe Johnny will now take my commands seriously."

"He is a good lad. I dislike being severe with the child so early in our acquaintance, but I believe he needed to have his boundaries established firmly. I hope you are right, that he will respect you from now on."

"He already adores you, Mr. Somerville. It almost seems that he admires you more because he fears your wrath."

"With boys this is often true. It brings to mind our relationship with the Lord. Would we respect Him if He did not occasionally remind us of His wrath and power? His love and tenderness are the more poignant because of His holiness and omnipotence. 'For whom the Lord loveth he chasteneth, and scourgeth every son whom he receiveth.' He has allotted me a 'scourging' or two when the need has arisen. At times I challenge His authority in my life just as Johnny challenged yours today."

Mercy regarded him with awe. "In what ways do you challenge His authority? I cannot imagine it. You seem wholly given over to His service and committed to doing His will, no matter what the consequences."

His hands slid up above her ankles, making it difficult for her to maintain clarity of thought.

Warren admitted soberly, "I have frequent conflicts of will with God, Mercy. They lessen in duration as I grow in maturity, thankfully, but since I tend to be headstrong, I fear this fault will not be entirely overcome until I reach glory."

"How does one argue with God? He does not speak aloud."

"How did you receive from Him the message that you should accept my offer of marriage?"

She paused to consider. "I prayed for wisdom and guidance. I knew somehow that this was meant to be, that it was God's will. I still wonder whether I was following God's leading, for my grandmother believed that I was making a mistake."

"And what did your father say?"

"He never forbade me to marry you, although he did set out the stipulation about Johnny in order to discourage you. It was odd. . ."

"What was odd?"

"Unlike Granny, he did not seem surprised or disappointed when you still chose to marry me. In fact, did you hear him mention something about a fleece when you declared your intent the other day?"

"Do you believe he was testing God and me to see if our

union was truly God's will?"

"Just as Gideon laid out the fleece and asked God to make it wet or dry." Tears pricked Mercy's eyes. "Pa does care about me and about Johnny. He is doing his best to provide for us." The assurance of her father's love melted much of the icy crust of hurt from her heart.

Warren's hands gently squeezed her ankles. "I am intensely grateful that you married me."

Her voice emerged as a croaking whisper. "What manner of woman did you expect me to be? When first we met, I mean."

He considered her question carefully before answering. "I do not know. I can truthfully say that I was agreeably surprised at our first meeting. I cannot begin to express my delight in your appearance, my dear; and in beauty of character, I believe you are everything any man could desire in his wife."

Although his compliments filled her with joy, she felt unworthy of them. "Yet I have ever so many faults; you know some of them."

"Frankly, I would be concerned if you had no faults, for then we would be ill matched indeed."

"But I do not understand what you want of me, how you want me to behave." Only a hint of the frustration she felt colored her voice, but Warren seemed to recognize it.

"My dear, do not worry yourself on that account. I desire that Mercy Somerville behave naturally, as Mercy Jones would behave. As far as housekeeping is concerned, we will resolve problems as we encounter them, I presume. Every newly married couple must. Doubtless, we shall frequently clash wills as we did this morning; nevertheless, I believe our love will survive occasional fits of pique or childishness on either side."

"But what about—what of private matters? My grandmother told me what a man requires of a wife, and you did not. . .I mean, last night. . ." Mercy shrank back into her seat corner, wishing she had never begun to ask.

He squeezed her feet gently. His gaze remained lowered, leaving her free to study his face. He seemed reluctant to answer, or perhaps he was choosing his words carefully. "Because I love you, Mercy, I will wait until you feel at ease in my presence. Our marriage will endure many, many years, Lord willing. I can and will consider your needs above my own; I have pledged it before God."

The muscles of his jaw worked for a moment. "I require only that you be equally candid. If anything I do or say offends you, tell me at once. Likewise, if anything pleases you, do not hesitate to inform me of the fact. I–I require encouragement; for I have little experience with women, and I cannot read your mind or your face with accuracy."

The coach jounced down a short incline. The horses splashed through a stream, and water drops appeared on the side windows. With both hands, Mercy braced herself against the jolts. Then the coach abruptly jerked to one side as though a wheel had dropped into a hole, and a terrible, grinding squeal made Mercy cover her ears.

Warren muttered something indistinct and threw the door open even before Oscar had brought the horses to a complete stop. "What did we hit?"

"There must have been a sink hole in the middle of that creek. We were going along fine; then all at once the bottom dropped out." After handing Johnny into Warren's waiting arms, Oscar swung down from his seat, and the two men bent to inspect the coach's undercarriage. "Want me to crawl under there and find the trouble?"

"Better unhitch the horses before you try it." Warren pulled out the step stool and addressed his wife. "Come out, my dear. It appears our delay will be of some duration."

After Warren helped her down, Mercy clung to her brother's hand and moved back to watch the men work. Her shoes were still uncomfortably damp.

Oscar and Warren had just tethered the three horses at the side of the road when, with a screech of rending metal, the coach sagged to one side. A wheel rolled gracefully to the roadside and settled into the dust, spinning to a stop. The horses tossed their heads and stamped nervously.

When the dust settled, Oscar and Warren exchanged glances. "The Lord preserved us today," Warren stated. "Had that axle broken while the coach moved, we might all have been killed. And had you crawled beneath, Oscar. . ."

"True. Nevertheless, I am responsible." Oscar's face was sober and drawn. "I inspected Mister Martin's work and pronounced the coach safe."

"You did not anticipate the condition of these roads," Warren observed. "For town driving, the coach undoubtedly would have been safe. I do not place blame upon you, my friend. Please do not take it upon yourself. Simply give thanks to God for his protection." Quietly, he slipped an arm around Mercy's shoulders. Johnny crept beneath his other arm.

Wind sighed through pine trees overhead and a few birds called in the stillness of the afternoon. Mercy felt her husband's fingers gripping her shoulder. He must wish to be home as profoundly as she wished it. "Now what shall we do, Mr. Somerville?" she asked.

"We have three healthy horses. We will push the coach off the road and ride home. We can return for our luggage and the coach Monday." With one last squeeze, he released her and headed toward the crippled carriage.

Oscar cleared his throat. "If I may make a suggestion?"

"What is it?" Warren asked with a touch of impatience. He had already begun to pull bags from the boot to remove essential items.

"Perhaps Miss Mercy, Johnny, and I should take lodging at the nearest inn while you ride ahead. That way you will not miss your meeting with the church board, and you could deliver your morning sermon before returning for us Monday."

"Where is the sense in that?" Warren scoffed. "It would be far better for all of us to arrive home tonight."

"But the coach horses are already tired, as are Johnny and

Miss Mercy. Riding without saddles would make an exhausting journey for a woman and a child."

Mercy silently agreed. The idea of a three- or four-hour bareback ride held no appeal.

Warren cast her an impatient glance as though reading her traitorous thoughts. "You would not wish me to leave, would you, Mercy?"

"No," she said quickly, then began to hedge, "Can we not all lodge in a nearby town until Monday? Johnny is weary, and I have no riding attire. Surely Oscar could mend the coach, and in a few days we can be on our way. I do not see the wisdom in abandoning our possessions—"

Warren cut her off. "I pledged to return for the meeting tonight and for service tomorrow. Staying is not an option."

"Yet we must adjust to altered circumstances," Mercy reminded him. "I believe Oscar is correct."

In the end, Warren had to agree. He rode ahead to a nearby town, hired a wagon, and returned for his family and their luggage. The town of Beaton's only lodging place was a decrepit tavern. Warren did not wish to leave his family there, yet he had little choice.

"These accommodations are adequate, Mr. Somerville. It is for only two nights, after all." Mercy assured her husband as he carried her trunk into the small upstairs room. Johnny had remained with Oscar to care for the horses.

Warren set the trunk on the floor and gave his humble surroundings a look of contempt. "Are you certain you could not ride to Beaufort with me tonight? The Colonel has carried us both before."

"Not such a distance. You know very well that we cannot ask it of him. And I could not leave Johnny and Oscar unprotected." She considered her own words and commented, "Does it not seem ludicrous that I must protect Oscar? Yet some wicked person could pronounce him a runaway, destroy his papers, and drive him off to a slave market if they were to discover him alone and unknown. It has happened before. I will protect him from harm as surely as he will protect Johnny and me."

Warren paced to the dingy window and looked down into Beaton Tavern's back lot. "I will leave my remaining cash funds with you, taking only the amount required to pay the ferryman."

"I also have my grandmother's jade ring, which I could sell if necessary."

Warren gave her a startled look. "I had not heard of this ring."

"As we prepared to leave home yesterday, Granny gave me a pouch. I did not know what it contained until much later." She pulled the small pouch from a pocket in her voluminous skirt, and extracted from it a gold ring. "It is valuable; I know."

Warren examined it by the window's light. Twinkling diamonds surrounded one large jadestone. "From where did it come?"

"It belonged to my grandmother's family, the Hardisons. Ugly, is it not?"

He gave her another surprised glance. "I would not display it openly until we are safely home."

"It is too large for my finger. Do you suppose it was intended for a man?"

"Perhaps."

"Would you like to have it? Granny probably expected me to give it to you."

He shook his head. "It is your treasure, my dear. I wear only my signet ring, no other."

"We could perhaps trade it for a new carriage?"

"No."

"But I wish to help, Mr. Somerville! This is my sole possession of value."

"Then save it until a time of great need. I would not have you sell a family heirloom for a lesser reason." He pressed it into her palm and closed her fingers around it.

Mercy looked down at their hands. "I wish you were not

obliged to leave us tonight, but I honor your commitment to duty."

"Honesty compels me to admit that duty alone would not drag me from your side this night, my wife. I must also procure for Oscar the materials to repair our carriage. They are unlikely to be found nearer than New Bern."

"And no mercantile will open until Monday," Mercy summarized their dilemma. "Do you have your sermon prepared for tomorrow?"

"Yes, my notes are in my office."

"This meeting you were so eager to attend, what is it?"

"The board members plan to review the first weeks of my ministry and discuss any issues that have arisen. They were most insistent upon my attendance."

"It sounds important. No wonder you were anxious to return in time. Will you now be too late?" Mercy stepped closer to him, longing to revive the closeness they had shared in the carriage that afternoon.

He lifted a hand and stroked her cheek with his fingertips. "This meeting is secondary to the well-being of my family. I could not hasten away, leaving you to endure unknown privations. We must trust the Lord to resolve the matter." His voice softened to a passionate murmur. "Mercy, it is difficult for me to leave you."

Mercy slid one hand up his chest. Her fingers brushed the whiskers on his neck, and she found the pulse beating in his throat. His thick brows and lashes tickled her fingers. Compared to that scratchy beard, his forehead and cheekbones felt silky smooth. Closing his eyes, he turned his face toward her hand. She slid her fingers down his long nose to find his parted lips. He kissed her fingers, and she gave a little gasp.

"Mercy, have mercy," he implored in a whisper.

Eagerly she lifted her face as he sought her lips. Warren's kisses filled her world. When he lifted his head, she tugged him back for more and felt rather than heard his helpless groan of protest. His trembling hands skimmed her body, sending waves of excitement and joy through her.

There was a knock at the door.

They froze, lips and bodies interlocked. Mercy's eyes popped open to meet Warren's startled gaze.

"Lefty? You in there?" Oscar's hesitant question drew them apart.

Mercy straightened her clothing and took deep, calming breaths. Warren grimaced, shaking his head, then gave Mercy a wry smile. "Yes, I am here." He opened the door.

Johnny lay fast asleep in Oscar's arms. "He dozed off in the barn. Uh, sorry to bother you." Oscar's brown eyes skipped between their faces. He quickly laid Johnny across the bed and backed out of the room.

When the door closed, Warren smiled at his wife, eyes twinkling although his smile held more than a hint of regret. "I must go. That was a timely, though unwelcome, reminder of my duty."

"Poor Oscar. And poor little Johnny." Mercy's voice was shaky, but she tried to look brave. "Do return to us soon."

Warren replaced his hat. "Remember our conversation in the carriage today?"

She nodded.

"You will tell me if anything I do displeases you?"

"I will. Do. . .do I displease you?" Sudden worry filled her voice and wrinkled her forehead.

He touched the tip of her nose with one finger. "Not in any way. Forget everything your Granny advised you, my dear, and behave with me exactly as you feel. Do you recall the purposes for which God provided marriage as enumerated during the wedding sermon yesterday? God declared that it was good. Not merely tolerable, you understand, but *good*. Bear that thought in mind, my wife."

She nodded meekly. "I do not embarrass you?"

"Not in any way. I adore you, Mercedes Somerville."

ten

Let your light so shine before men, that they may see your good works, and glorify your Father which is in heaven.
Matthew 5:16

It was after nine o'clock when Warren halted the Colonel outside Beauregard Reynolds' house. A liveried stable boy came to lead the horse away. "Want that I should walk 'im awhile before he gets a drink?" he asked, studying the gelding's lathered shoulders.

"Yes, thank you, until he is cool." Then Warren gave the child a second glance. "Why are you out at this hour? Time for children to be in bed."

"The master told me to stay up until all the gen'lemen left. I'll get to sleep in tomorrow. I'm 'leven; I ain' no child."

Sadly, Warren realized that the boy's childhood in all likelihood had already ended. "I shall endeavor to be precipitate."

The boy gave him a blank stare. "I'm thinkin' you looks fine just like you is, suh. Some other gen'lemen got here just before you did, Mistah Preacher."

Warren's brows lifted. Brushing off his dusty boots with an equally dusty glove, he considered the effect his disheveled appearance might have upon the church board. *Perhaps I ought to have stopped home and changed first. Too late for second guesses.*

Moments later, he was ushered into a richly paneled library. A fire blazed upon the hearth, its flickering light revealing extensive collections of books, butterflies, and silhouettes. Six men observed Warren over the cut crystal glasses they had been drinking from. His host ordered in a gruff Southern drawl, "Take a seat, Preacher. We have not yet begun the meeting. Pompey, pour the preacher a glass of port."

"No, thank you, Pompey." Warren lifted a hand politely to the elderly servant. "I apologize for my tardy and dusty appearance, gentlemen. I have ridden long and hard to attend this meeting. Unavoidable circumstances caused the delay." A gray-bearded man seated in the shadows caught his eye, and Warren brightened. "Uncle Wyeth! It is good to see you, sir."

"And you, my boy." His uncle rose partway to accept Warren's handshake. "I have heard much about you since our return to town. You have been a busy young man."

Mr. Carson, a prosperous businessman, pushed his way into the conversation. "When you took leave of me the other night, Reverend Somerville, you promised to return to town in plenty of time for this meeting. It does not give the right appearance, a preacher who gallops about the countryside and dresses like a tulip of fashion. Why can you not wear vestments and drive a gig as a respectable parson should?"

"I rather like the effect of a virile preacher," another man opined. "Too often, men are inclined to find Christianity effeminate. Our parson puts the lie to that notion."

"West, you're missing the point," Carson sneered. "Can you imagine Christ riding a blooded hack about, dressed to the nines? I think not. A minister needs to portray godly humility in his manner and his attire. That waistcoat alone must have cost a week's wages," he waved a languid hand toward Warren's midsection.

Nathan Wyeth's chuckle drew all eyes to his corner. "As you can see, my boy, your activities have been the topic of much discussion. Why don't you take yourself a seat here and set back to listen a spell?"

Warren pulled up a chair and sat down, feeling something like a man before a firing line. The other men all seemed to talk at once, voicing their varied opinions.

"Another thing," Reynolds's deep voice cut through the lesser conversations. "I hear that the boy's sermons are too harsh. Less talk about sin and repentance is what we require.

We don't mind hearing about heaven and how to praise the Almighty, but there's no call to lay guilt on people."

"I thoroughly enjoyed the sermon last Sunday," Dionysius West, the town barber and doctor, dared again to disagree. "It does people good to be shaken up at times. We could use some repentance and reformation in this town. The other preachers don't dare talk about it. I had hoped that Reverend Somerville here would be man enough to put out the whole gospel message; I have not been disappointed. If we are not sinners, why do we need a Savior?"

"Amen," Warren inserted, scooting back in his deep chair. Reynolds gave him a quelling look and Carson snorted. Orville Draper, a planter, and Horace Moore, a lawyer, listened and sipped their drinks, content to let the others quarrel among themselves.

Pompey refilled crystal glasses as they were emptied. Warren watched the dignified servant and wondered what he was thinking.

"And what do you say about that, young man?" Carson addressed Warren sharply.

"About what, sir?" Warren started back to attention. "I am sorry. It has been a trying day."

"So trying that you cannot pay attention to our discussion?" Carson shook his balding head. "This meeting could decide your future, you know. We were discussing the issue of servants. We have decided that it would be a good thing if you were to take on a household servant. Then you would not have to associate with undesirables at that boarding house."

"I could hire you a housekeeper for minimal cost," Reynolds offered in his patronizing way. "A slave who can cook and clean is what you need."

"I will soon have a hired servant in my home," Warren announced calmly. "He and my wife and her young brother will be arriving Monday. They were obliged to stay behind today when our carriage broke down."

"Your wife?" Nathan Wyeth nearly swallowed his pipe.

"Yes, Uncle Wyeth. I was married yesterday morning to the sister of an old friend. I will be pleased to present Mrs. Somerville to you at my earliest opportunity."

"Why, congratulations, my boy!" Dr. West finally broke the shocked silence.

The others joined in with genuine, albeit subdued, felicitations. Wyeth cleared his throat before adding wryly, "Your aunt will be sorely disappointed, son. She had anticipated introducing you to several eligible local belles. But perhaps she will take to your wife and enjoy launching her into society. She always wanted a daughter."

"It would please me if Aunt Wyeth welcomed my wife. Mrs. Somerville will be in need of sympathetic feminine companionship, no doubt."

Reynolds cleared his throat. "That settles it. Your wife will certainly expect servants. I just had an inspiration: I will donate a servant's labor and take the fee out of my tithe. You will likely need a manservant, too."

"Thank you for your generous offer, but I do not desire a maidservant. And, as aforementioned, I already have a hired manservant."

Carson bluntly inquired about this servant's race.

"My servant and friend has dark skin, yes. He has been a free man for many years."

The flat statements caused a general gasp.

"Mr. Somerville, I believe you and I need to have a private talk," Nathan Wyeth stated. "There are evidently many things about your situation that you don't fully understand. Gentlemen," he addressed his compatriots, "I request this meeting be adjourned until perhaps three days hence? These differences are not insurmountable. My nephew is young and impetuous, but he is also wise, respectful, and able to work out some sort of compromise."

"That remains to be seen," Carson snapped and snarled a derisive oath.

Dr. West rose to pace across the room. He tapped ash from

his pipe into the tray Pompey offered. "What I have seen already is a marked increase in attendance and interest since this young man first addressed our church. Only two sermons so far, yet several people have mentioned to me their eager anticipation regarding the next. I cannot recall hearing such remarks in the past about any other preacher. Can you?"

It must have been a rhetorical question, for no one responded.

"Our fledgling chapel, made up of misfits and dissidents, is now offering rich spiritual food to residents of Beaufort—all because of this one young man and his honest desire to preach God's Word. I think it is utterly superb, and for my part, I say 'Bravo, Somerville. Keep up the good work.' "

"Hear, hear." Draper finally spoke up.

When the meeting adjourned, Nathan Wyeth accompanied Warren to the parsonage. "I do not believe you understand the gravity of your position, my boy," he persisted. "Your appointment here was somewhat provisional from the outset, and this attitude of yours regarding slavery is rendering it nothing short of precarious. Reynolds and Carson wish to replace you, and I fear that Captain Nottingham will agree with them when he returns from this voyage. The other three support you at this time, but their votes could easily change."

"Uncle Wyeth, I appreciate your concern, and I am grateful for your support. It will please me to see you and Aunt Wyeth in church tomorrow. I have noticed that several of the church board members do not regularly attend. Mr. Reynolds' health prevents his attendance, no doubt."

"Yes, but he does provide vital financial support and wise guidance. The captain is presently at sea, of course. The other four men attend faithfully. These six men are the cornerstones of the church, I must remind you, and your salary largely comes out of their contributions."

"Ah, but you are forgetting that the Stone the builders rejected became the Chief Cornerstone. My position here and my salary are provided by the Lord, not by any man. The Lord has used these fine men to accomplish His plans, but He does not depend upon them, and neither do I."

Nathan's forehead wrinkled. "Somerville, you are being remarkably short-sighted. I must admit feeling somewhat put out about your sudden marriage. You might at least have warned your aunt and me. Nonetheless, we are prepared to accept your bride and introduce you both into the best society in these parts—nothing compared to that which you no doubt enjoyed in England, but fine society still. Your Aunt Wyeth will undoubtedly wish to give you a grand reception."

"This is kind of you, Uncle—"

"I have not yet finished. You must learn, son, to distinguish between those issues that must be carried through and those on which you might compromise for the purpose of maintaining a necessary peace and balance."

"I entirely concur."

"Let me finish, please. Tonight you were offered—a generous offer, let me point out—the services of two of Reynolds' people. I have never known the man to make such an overture before. He was extending the right hand of fellowship, yet twice—*twice,* mind you—that offer was rejected. Are you so determined to make enemies that you cannot bend your own plans to accommodate an important man?"

"No, sir. I did entirely appreciate the motive behind his offer. He was testing me, sir, and I did not intend to fail that test."

"Nonsense! By refusing his offer, you most certainly did fail the most vital of tests—the measure of respect you bear your elders!" Nathan's shout echoed off the parsonage walls and rang along the silent street. "I expect he will make the offer one last time, and for your own well-being, I would advise you to accept. Consider your ways, my boy."

Dismounting before his stable, Warren said flatly, "Uncle Wyeth, it is late, and I am in dire need of sleep. I would ask you to come inside, but I do not think I could long remain awake as your host."

"Mrs. Wyeth will be looking for me anyway," Nathan admitted, settling back into his saddle like a bird smoothing its ruffled feathers. "We will be in the service tomorrow. Preach a good sermon, my boy, if you want to keep West on your side. Dissecting sermons is his favorite pastime. I am interested to hear what manner of preaching has met with his approval."

"I shall preach the sermon God has laid upon my heart," Warren promised. "His is the only approval I seek." He headed the Colonel toward the stable. "Good night, Uncle Wyeth, and thank you for your thoughtfulness. I am grateful and thankful to have family near."

Nathan turned his horse, then reined back. "I hope you understand that I am not angry about your marriage, my boy. I look forward to meeting your bride. Where did you say she is tonight?"

Warren briefly explained the events of his day.

Nathan Wyeth studied his horse's mane, mulling over this information, then announced, "I think it would be wiser, under the circumstances, if we were to bring your coach here for repairs."

Warren protested, "My servant is a skilled blacksmith, and he—"

Wyeth lifted his hand. "Be that as it may, I would advise you to bring the carriage here and arrange its complete repair under more propitious circumstances and without the constraints of time. I will ride out with you, bringing a coach and a spare axle. I have skilled smiths at my plantation. I will send for two of them to accompany us."

"I shall be grateful for your company and aid," Warren answered honestly. "It is a long and lonely ride. Good night, Uncle Wyeth, and thank you for your help and support." Lifting a hand in farewell, Warren led his horse toward the dark stable.

≈

Just before opening the morning service with prayer, Warren let his gaze drift across the congregation. He returned a few smiles and nods, and felt budding affection for his flock as a whole. "It is good to see each one of you today. I am beginning to recognize faces, and even to connect them with names. Whether or not they are the correct names, time will tell us."

There was a slight ripple of startled laughter. Levity in church was unexpected.

"This is a time of great joy for God's people; the time of year when we remember our Lord's Advent upon this earth. It is a familiar story to most of us, this story of a baby's birth, and yet I will tell it today as though for the first time. Why? Because the wonder of God's condescension, His mercy, and His wondrous love can never, never grow old. God became man and dwelt among us! Glory to God in the highest, and on earth, peace, good will towards men." As he spoke the last line, Warren lifted his hands in thanksgiving and closed his eyes in prayer.

"Lord God, I humbly ask that You will open the hearts of these, Your sheep, to hear Your Word and believe in Jesus, Your perfect Christmas gift. I ask this in His name."

A hearty "Amen, Lawd!" echoed through the sanctuary. Startled, Warren glanced upward. Horatio's encouraging smile gleamed from the shadowy balcony.

Warren nodded, ignoring the uncomfortable murmur from the congregation. "Amen, indeed." Then he placed his hands upon the lectern, looked straight into Dionysius West's twinkling eyes, and began. "Once long ago, in a small town called Nazareth, there lived a humble maiden named Mary. . ."

હ

Beauregard Reynolds hobbled through the church door, followed closely by his wife and daughters. "We'd take it kindly if you'd join us for dinnah today, Reverend." Warren was about to gracefully refuse, when he noticed how the small woman's faded eyes begged his acceptance.

"I would be delighted, madam," he accepted without another thought.

"Jes' come right on ovah once you're finished heah," Mrs. Reynolds instructed. Her tiny hand tightened its grip on his hand. "We're in no rush."

Her husband nodded coldly without letting go of his cane or his Bible. The two daughters dropped tiny curtseys in return to Warren's bow.

Jonathan Munfrees and his mother waited patiently for Warren's notice. "That was a great story today, Reverend," the boy spoke boldly, pumping Warren's hand. "I never thought much about angels before, but when you told about them singing in the sky, I could almost hear them! I like church."

After the boy hurried down the steps to greet a friend, his mother quietly told Warren, "Jonathan was never interested in God until you came, Reverend. I don't know how to thank you. His father and I wanted to raise him Christian, but since my Joseph's ship was lost last winter, Jonathan has wanted nothing to do with God. He came to church with me that first week only because a friend told him that you rode a blooded hack and had an excellent seat. You see, the boy lives and breathes horses."

Warren listened in humble surprise. "I was unaware of your widowed state, Mrs. Munfrees. Perhaps my wife and I may visit you and Jonathan sometime soon. I would like to become better acquainted with the boy."

The woman's eyes filled with tears. "You are an answer to many prayers, Reverend Somerville. I can see Jesus in you whenever you stand up to speak in church. I can see Him in your eyes even now."

Warren swallowed hard. "There is no greater honor than to represent Him, Mrs. Munfrees."

❧

The new church's first evening service was good, although the attendance was sparse. Warren started the evening with singing, selecting the brightest, most cheerful hymns he knew. The loft was nearly empty, for many servants were not allowed more than one service a week. Warren missed Bonny's hearty singing voice. He then asked for prayer requests, but only one elderly man, Mr. Hampton, lifted his hand to request prayer for his "rheumatiz." The short sermon about the wise men who traveled far to search for Jesus seemed to capture the audience's attention, and Warren felt reasonably satisfied with his first evening service.

He left the darkened church and returned to the parsonage. The house was dark and lonely even after he stirred the fire and lit a lamp.

He was hungry. Carrying the lamp, Warren walked out to the detached kitchen and scavenged for something to eat. He found only stale corn pone and a bin of apples. There was little for Mercy to work with when she arrived, he realized.

Returning to the main house, he began to prepare for bed. Something bumped against his leg when he removed his coat. Reaching into the pocket, he found his Christmas gift. A lovely aroma reached his nose as he lifted the little sack in one hand. Loosening the drawstring, he peeked inside. The brown crust of a small raisin-speckled loaf met his eyes.

Moments later, as he picked the last few crumbs from the bottom of the sack, he remembered to thank the Lord for His timely provision and for a kindly woman who had foreseen his need.

Climbing once again into his cold bed, he lay with open eyes, trying to recall the warm curves of Mercy's body, the fervor of her kisses. Had she really kissed him with such abandon, or had it been a dream contrived of his frustrated desire? Already, the precious memories were fading.

A familiar ache remained in his heart, the lonely longing for his wife's love. "She spoke my name once, Lord," he groaned aloud. "Yesterday she kissed me and seemed to enjoy my caresses. Lord, forgive my impatience, but I want more. I want her to love me as entirely, as desperately as I love her. I beseech You, grant me Mercy!"

❧

The ride back to Beaton seemed interminable to Warren; although, his uncle's company and conversation provided a welcome distraction. Behind them, a coach rumbled along the bumpy road, its matched bays driven by a strapping slave who never smiled. A younger man perched beside him, letting the meager winter sunshine warm his nut-brown face.

The coach's attendance slowed their pace, which annoyed Warren; yet he knew that the extra vehicle might prove necessary if his carriage could not be quickly prepared for travel. Not for the first time, he regretted purchasing Martin Jones's "bargain."

Had he not been yearning to reach Mercy, he might have enjoyed that ride. He and Wyeth wrangled for hours about various Scripture passages and how they related to the sensitive subject of slavery.

"If God had not intended that some men should serve others, He would not have inspired Paul to write precise instructions regarding slaves. Down through history, since the dawn of mankind, races have struggled for dominance. Look at the Greeks, the Romans, the Mongols, and the barbarians. Tell me that history has not always contained a ruling class and a servant class! You see? You cannot!" Nathan expostulated.

Warren countered, "Yet the Scriptures also give instructions for divorce. Does this mean that God intended divorce to be a normal part of human experience? Not in the least. God's allowance for human weakness does not excuse our sin. Paul did not endorse slavery, although he frequently used it as an analogy to our sinful natural condition. He would, I am certain, have rather practiced and preached Christ's Golden Rule: 'Do unto others as you would have them do unto you.' If you cannot honestly say that you would wish to be treated as your slaves are treated, then you are not living by that rule."

Nathan's mouth opened twice; each time he closed it to rethink his position and his ensuing remark. "Some slaves choose to remain with their masters even when given the choice, my boy. You cannot think that Horatio and Bonny would prefer to live on their own! If given a choice, they would certainly choose life at Wyeth House over a daily struggle to survive. I treat my people well, and they are happy to serve me."

"Always? You have never owned a malcontent?"

Nathan brushed this aside. "Not to speak of. I don't allow my overseer to whip unless the infraction is major. Our people are treated well—like children, if you will. They are valuable possessions, not to be abused."

Shaking his head in disbelief, Warren countered, "Uncle, if given the choice, they may very well choose to remain with you; this is true. But do you not see how much it would mean to them to be given that choice? What must a man feel in his soul when he knows that he has no say regarding his future? How is it to know that one's wife and children belong to another man? Can you not put yourself into that position for only a moment and sympathize with their plight?"

Wyeth was silent. His mare tossed her head as though her rider had sent mixed signals. At length, he said, "You cannot understand our position, Somerville. This is our way of life, our subsistence. If you threaten slavery, you threaten a Southerner's existence. Take care, my boy. Your position is a dangerous one in these parts. You may stand to lose more than your employment should you persist in this manner of thinking."

Warren could hardly believe his ears. "You threaten me?"

"I would not threaten my own sister's son. I am no danger to you, but others will not be as forgiving as I. Though I fear that I cast my pearls before swine, I offer this valuable advice: Buy yourself a servant. You may treat the creature as kindly as you wish—you may even quietly free it at some later date. In this way, you would prove beyond doubt that you bear no grudge against those of your flock that own servants. Try to find it in your heart to commiserate not with slaves, but with your own kind who are in need of your ministry. I was deeply impressed by your sermons yesterday. You have a gift, my son. Use it as God intended; do not allow your ministry in Beaufort to be destroyed by an unreasoning crusade against our traditions!"

Warren felt blood roaring through his veins. His forehead throbbed with the effort of containing violent wrath. "Sir, God originally created only one race—the human race. I believe that all human beings are my 'kind.' I appreciate the concern which prompts your advice, but I can assure you with absolute confidence that I will never, ever own a slave."

His uncle sighed. "I expected this reply. I will continue to pray that God will soften your heart in this regard, Somerville, my boy. Such a disappointment! In many ways, you did seem to be the ideal minister for our little chapel."

Warren maintained a chilly silence for the short remainder of their journey. The very idea that his uncle dared to pray for God to change Warren's mind infuriated the young preacher anew.

When the sun-faded rooftops of Beaton hove into view, Warren's heart seemed to expand within his chest. "This is the town," he informed Wyeth shortly.

His eyes scanned the empty tavern windows even as he dismounted. Anxiety accelerated his heartbeat. Was Mercy still here? Without waiting for his uncle, he rushed inside. The proprietor entered the lobby from another doorway. "Can I help—Oh, it's you, sir. Your wife and the boy ain't here right now—"

Warren grabbed the man by the shirtfront with both hands and demanded, "Where is she?"

"Calm down, mister, and give me a chance to answer. She's down at the livery stable with that slave—Hey, mister!" But Warren was gone.

Flinging into the Colonel's saddle, he barked a short explanation to his uncle, wheeled the horse, and galloped him toward the livery. As he approached, Mercy emerged from a side door, shading her eyes against the late morning sunlight. Before the Colonel came to a complete stop, Warren was on the ground with his wife in his arms, heedless of watching eyes.

She hugged him back for a moment, then pushed away. "Oh, Mr. Somerville, you won't believe what all has happened to us—"

"Warren!" he groaned. "Please, please call me Warren again." Although she was noticeably disheveled and untidy, the sight, feel, and scent of her delighted his heart. "What have you been doing? Oh, darling, how I have missed you!"

He tried to pull her closer, but she resisted. "Mr. Somerville—Warren, there are people watching us," she murmured, glancing around. "Is this man your uncle?"

Returning to his senses, Warren reluctantly released his wife and straightened his coat. "Yes, my dear. Mercy, may I present my uncle Nathan Wyeth. Uncle, this is my wife, Mercedes Somerville."

Wyeth had been observing the reunion with an indulgent expression. Now he stepped forward to accept Mercy's offered hand. "Welcome to the family, Mrs. Somerville. I can now appreciate the reason for my nephew's zeal to return in haste."

Mercy returned his smile, yet she seemed distracted. At the earliest opportunity, she asked Warren if she could speak with him in private.

"In a moment. We must begin upon our business here if we are to return to Beaufort tonight. Where is Oscar?"

"He is inside. Mister. . .Warren, this is of utmost importance."

Her earnest expression at last impressed him. "What is it?"

Taking him by the sleeve, she moved closer to the stable door. Wyeth politely moved back to his horse and loosened its cinch.

Mercy chewed her lower lip and looked deeply concerned. "I hope you will not be angry, but I did not know what else to do. You did say that my ring was to be sold only in an emergency, and I cannot see how anything could be more urgent than—"

"Mercy, what has happened?" Warren took her upper arms in his hands and gently squeezed. "Did that skinflint of a tavern keeper try to cheat you—"

"No, he did nothing wrong, really. It was a fair enough trade, I believe. I don't know how we are going to care for them, and Oscar is furious with me, but oh, Warren, I had to do something!"

Warren shook her gently. "Darling, what have you done?"

"I bought a slave. Actually, I bought two."

"You did *WHAT?*"

eleven

For the wrath of man worketh not the righteousness of God.
James 1:20

Mercy cringed. Warren's expression had instantly transformed from tender indulgence to horror. He dropped her arms as though they had burned him and staggered back two paces.

"I feared you would be angry, but I did not know what else to do. You see, she ran away last week and was caught and whipped, and then she developed a high fever and went into labor. She was so ill, and no one wanted to help her. I think they were planning to let her die because she has caused them too much trouble. Mr. Wallace would not allow me to go near her for fear she would harm me and then he would have to make account to you—so I traded my ring for her. Now she is our responsibility." Mercy explained as quickly as possible, hoping to erase the animosity from her husband's face. "Her name is Naomi, and she gave birth to a baby girl last night—I assisted at the birth, and oh, Warren, the baby is so precious! Oscar is upset with me now, although he did help me with the baby during the night."

Warren's expression did not soften. If anything, it became more remote.

A strange sputtering noise drew Mercy's gaze beyond Warren's frozen countenance. Nathan Wyeth leaned against his horse's saddle, his face buried in one arm. The man's shoulders were shaking. Was he laughing at her? Mercy's lips trembled, and the knot in her stomach tightened.

Mercy approached her husband and laid one hand upon his chest. "Warren, please, won't you help me with her? Naomi is

141

in great need of love and compassion. Dinah, the cook at the tavern, told me that she has had a terribly tragic life. I believe we can help her to get well, and I am sure that God brought us into her life for a purpose—although she does not share that opinion."

Warren flinched from her touch. Silently, he turned on his heel, flung himself upon the Colonel's back, and rode out of town. As she watched him go, Mercy felt as though a blanket of security had been ripped from her back. Only then did she realize how totally she had come to depend upon Warren's love.

"I guess you were right, Oscar," Johnny's awed voice spoke from behind her. "Lefty sure is angry. Did you see how gray his face got?"

Turning slowly, Mercy faced Oscar and Johnny, who stood side by side in the stable doorway, watching Warren's figure disappear beyond the town limits. Mercy stared into Oscar's face. His anger must have cooled when Warren's flared, for now she saw only gentle pity in his brown eyes. "Oh, Oscar, what can I do?" Covering her face with both hands, she began to weep.

"Well, missy, we must make the best of the situation. I don't know how you're going to reconcile with Lefty; that's your concern. When he calms down, he will agree that we cannot abandon a mother and child and pretend nothing happened. Whether we would or no, they are now our responsibility."

Johnny ran to hug his sister, alarmed by her tears. "It's scary when Mr. Somerville gets mad at you, isn't it?" he commiserated. "He still loves you even when he's angry, Mercy. He told me so."

Mercy gratefully hugged her little brother. It felt good to be held, even by a child. "I hope you're right, Johnny. Oh, Mr. Wyeth, this is our friend and servant Oscar Dunn, who is an expert blacksmith. Oscar, this is my husband's uncle."

"Ah, yes. My nephew has spoken of you." Wyeth did not offer to shake Oscar's hand, but the big man took no offense.

"I brought along two of my smiths, a spare axle, and materials that should prove sufficient for at least temporary repairs."

"And I have spoken with the town smith about using his forge. He is reluctant but willing to allow us the use of it." Oscar walked alongside Wyeth's horse. Turning back, he commanded sternly: "You care for that woman and child, Miss Mercy. Johnny, you help your sister. I shall fix the coach and have a talk with Lefty. Keep praying, you hear me?"

Mercy nodded, her face and eyes still moist and pink. "Thank you, Oscar."

❧

The baby was sleeping, so Mercy checked on the mother. Naomi's smooth forehead was still hot, but she appeared to rest peacefully.

"I'm hungry, Mercy. So is Buttons."

Johnny's whisper sounded very loud. Mercy touched her lips with a warning finger. "Hush. I'll go ask at the tavern. You stay here and be very quiet."

He nodded, slid his back down the stable wall, and settled on a pile of dirty hay. The beagle nestled her head in his lap.

When Mercy returned with two plates piled with bacon, biscuits, fried greens, apple fritters, and chunks of shoofly pie, she heard the baby crying. Johnny rushed through the doorway and nearly upset her. "You're back! What took you so long? That baby is screaming, and I dunno what to do." He snatched a fritter from one plate and followed his sister into the small, musty room.

Naomi's eyes were open. She glanced at Mercy, then returned her blank stare to the ceiling.

"I brought food for all of us," Mercy announced, trying to sound cheerful. "And Dinah sent along clean rags for diapers. Poor little one! I shall hurry and clean you up, so you can eat, too," she tried to soothe the shrieking baby.

Naomi accepted a plate and ate hungrily, leaving the other plate for Johnny and Mercy.

"Johnny, would you please fetch us some fresh water in the

bucket? Dinah told me that Naomi needs to drink a lot."

While Johnny was away, Mercy quickly unwrapped the baby, wiped her clean, and bundled her into fresh clothing. "You sweet dolly," she murmured as the tiny mite squalled, seeking nourishment with open mouth like a baby bird. Strong little limbs kicked and flailed aimlessly, but Mercy handled the baby with experienced hands. "Just a moment, and you'll have your mummy. You need to let her eat first, you know, so she'll have lots of food for little ol' you."

Still chewing, Naomi set aside the plate and accepted her daughter. She neither looked at Mercy nor acknowledged her presence in any way. Mercy told her to call if she needed anything, then escorted Johnny from the room. He ate from his plate as he walked, occasionally dropping bits for the eager Buttons.

The two perched atop barrels near the storeroom doorway. "I wonder where Mr. Somerville went," Johnny remarked, setting the empty plate beside him on the barrel.

Mercy rescued it before it could fall and shatter. "I don't know. Have you been praying like Oscar told us?"

"No. Have you?"

"I've been so busy, I forgot. Would you like to pray with me now?"

"Out loud? Right here?"

"No one is listening to us except God."

"What about her?" Johnny jerked a thumb toward the storeroom.

"It does not matter if she hears us. She is family now, anyway."

Johnny gave his sister an odd look, but obediently bowed his head.

Mercy folded her hands and bowed her head. "Dear Lord, as You know, we are in a dreadful dilemma here. I thank You for leading us to Naomi and her precious baby, and I ask for Your healing touch on her body and her soul. Please help Oscar as he speaks with Mr. Somerville today. Give him wisdom and understanding, and please open my husband's heart to see how much Naomi needs our help."

Mercy's voice broke. She could not speak her greatest desire aloud, but her heart cried, *Oh, Lord, please make Warren love me again!* "We request these things in the name of Jesus."

"Amen," Johnny said in his deepest voice.

❧

Oscar reined in his puffing gray gelding and waited in the road while the Colonel trotted toward him. Warren refused to meet his friend's penetrating eyes.

"We have repaired the coach. Everyone is waiting to travel on. Where have you been, Lefty?"

"Thinking." Warren allowed Oscar to fall in beside him.

"I hope you have also been praying, my friend."

Warren sighed deeply and gave the other man a quick glance. "What shall I do? I have sworn before the Lord never to own a human being, yet as soon as I leave my wife alone, she purchases a slave! I would have trusted her with my very life—and she has betrayed that trust at her first opportunity!"

Oscar quoted gently, "'Let every man be swift to hear, slow to speak, slow to wrath.' You must consider this situation carefully and prayerfully before arriving at a plan of procedure. You know that God must have a plan for this—"

Warren let out a disgusted huff and halted his horse sharply. "A plan for Mercy to buy a slave? You, of all people, can say this? She told me you were angry with her, too, yet now you lecture me about holding my wrath in check."

Oscar also stopped and looked squarely into his friend's cold eyes. "I knew that you would disapprove of her actions and I advised your wife accordingly. However, when I first learned of the situation, it was already too late to intervene: the purchase had been transacted. This Naomi is a strong, bitter, wretched woman, and she struck at anyone who approached her that first night. I feared for your wife's safety."

"How did Mercy come to find her?"

"I believe she was awakened by the woman's screams. I can only apologize that I did not keep closer watch over your wife during your absence, Lefty. She slipped out of her room without my knowledge, since I was in the livery stable at the time."

Warren shook his head. "I do not hold you accountable for this in any way. I know without being told that you did not neglect your duty. It is Mercy—that heedless, impulsive, bull-headed. . ." He sputtered for a moment. "I want to shake her and embrace her, shout at her and. . ."

"I understand." Oscar repressed a smile. "If it is any comfort, Johnny did not awaken that first night, and he has not often been in the slave woman's objectionable company. I understand your Mercy's desire to—to show mercy, yet I could wish that she had chosen a more prepossessing and grateful object for her mercy."

While his horse dozed off, Warren slumped in the saddle, his hands resting limply on the pommel. "What am I to do?"

"Your wife seems adept at practicing her faith, showing love to the unlovable. You and I both could learn from her." Oscar's broad forehead wrinkled as he considered his next words. "Tell me, had you and your uncle been having words before you reached town today?"

Warren lifted one brow to inspect his friend's expression. "Yes."

"On the subject of slavery?"

Warren nodded shortly. "Heated words."

There was a pause before Oscar's next query. "Are you certain your current anger is not at least partially based upon thwarted pride?"

Warren straightened abruptly, eyes flashing.

"I trust in our friendship and in the Lord's healing power that my words will not drive us apart." Oscar's eyes were deadly serious. "Lefty, you seem eager to confront your peers regarding the issue of slavery. While I appreciate your concern and empathy more than I can express, I am troubled by your approach to the problem. Are you certain that the indignation you feel is God's righteous anger? While it is true that my race frequently experiences hatred and lack of acceptance even from professed Christians, it is also true that retaliation and return of that hatred will not improve our lot in life. Only the Holy Spirit can change men's hearts; you cannot force them to change."

Warren stared blankly at Oscar's face. His gray eyes were wide, shocked.

"In your well-meaning effort to single-handedly balance out the injustices we black people have experienced, it is possible that you are becoming unbalanced in yourself. I do not advise you to overlook or condone sin in your congregation; I merely remind you to love the sinners and allow God to change their hearts."

Warren protested, "Oscar, had you heard my uncle pledge to pray that God would soften my heart toward slavery, you would understand my fury!"

"Believe me, my friend: I do understand your fury. Do you not know that each day, each hour, I must beg my Lord to give me love and forgiveness for my fellow man?"

Staring into the other man's fathomless eyes, Warren swallowed hard and blinked. Although rocked by the power of Oscar's testimony, he still objected weakly, "You are not free to speak as I am. God has placed me in a position where I must preach the truth! Even Jesus was angered by sin; how can I keep silent while travesties of the truth are bandied about by supposed Christians?"

Oscar's face expressed sympathy. "I did not recommend silence, Lefty. Certainly God intends to use You to feed His sheep in Beaufort. Yet, although your intentions are good, you must always keep in mind that the devil's best ploys involve twisting something good into something evil. A combative spirit, strife, and a bitter tongue cannot coexist in your life with a humble spirit, a joyful heart, and a praising tongue. Remember the Apostle James's words: 'Doth a fountain send forth at the same place sweet water and bitter?' We are commanded to 'speak the truth *in love.*'"

After a moment of ringing silence, he added, "Returning to the origin of this conversation, I believe your anger with your wife is exaggerated, and perhaps. . .misdirected."

Warren's chest heaved with repressed emotions. Unable to speak, he wheeled his horse around and continued into town.

๛

Mercy peered out of the small, foggy side window of the old coach, following her husband's figure with longing eyes. He sat tall and straight upon his horse, eyes ahead. Her lips quivered and her eyes filled. "Oh, Warren," she breathed silently.

He had returned to town with Oscar, but in spite of Mercy's earnest prayers, all was not yet right. Warren had soberly issued and received instructions, working alongside the other men until the small cavalcade headed out of Beaton toward Beaufort. Mercy rode with Naomi and the baby in the repaired coach with Oscar driving; Johnny and Buttons rode with Nathan Wyeth in the other carriage with the two slaves driving. Warren rode beside his wife's carriage, but he never once looked her way.

As she settled back in her seat, Mercy glanced up to meet Naomi's keen gaze. "Your man's mad at you." It was the first time Naomi had either looked directly at her or spoken anything other than a curse.

Mercy nodded. "He is angry with me for buying you. I feel terrible—but I would have felt worse had I left you with that dreadful man who wanted you to die."

Naomi said no more. Shifting the baby to her other breast, she gave Mercy another glance. For an instant, Mercy thought she recognized some softness or emotion in the other woman's eyes.

"God will bring good out of all this; I know it." Mercy wished she felt as certain as she sounded.

twelve

Gently, he hefted his wife's limp form into his arms. The task
was made difficult not only by the coach's cramped quarters,
but also by his aching hip and leg.

"I can do that, Lefty. You must be nearly exhausted," Oscar
protested.

"I will carry my own wife," Warren growled. Mercy's head
bumped against his shoulder, and she groaned softly. She did
not smell sweet and clean anymore, he noticed. Hardly surpris-
ing, considering what she had been doing for the past few days.

As Warren limped up the path leading to the parsonage's
front door, Nathan Wyeth descended the inside staircase,
returning from carrying Johnny to his bed. He held the door
open. Warren felt Oscar's hovering presence at his back. He
reached the base of the steps and realized the impossibility of
carrying Mercy any farther. Exhausted, annoyed, aching, he
simply stood there and glared at the steps.

Suddenly, Oscar's hands clutched Warren's elbows from
behind. "Hold on," the big man warned. Startled, Warren
stiffened his arms, and Oscar lifted him and Mercy to the top
step in one quick rush. Warren met his uncle's laughing eyes
and silently dared him to remark. Nathan Wyeth merely lifted
his brows and grinned.

While making his tedious way down the hall to the bedroom
doorway, Warren first heard angry voices from outside, then a
baby's wail. He glanced back in time to see Naomi stiffly
climbing the porch steps. Her expression was icy. Oscar

149

followed her closely, carrying her whimpering baby. The man bore a startling resemblance to a thundercloud, dark and menacing. *The woman must have a tongue like a razor blade if she can irritate Oscar,* Warren mused.

"Miss Naomi," Warren said just loudly enough to gain her attention, "you may have the room to the left at the top of the stairs. If you need anything tonight, please ask Mr. Dunn or me."

She gave him the merest nod and began to ascend the stairs.

"I shall return home now, my boy," Nathan announced to Warren's back. "I imagine Mrs. Wyeth will come to greet your bride on the morrow. I do wish you all joy in your future." Although his voice held suppressed mirth, it was sincere.

Warren turned at his doorway and nodded in farewell. His anger was rapidly fading. There did not seem to be much point in fostering animosity toward everyone who countered his opinions. It was unpleasant to be an object of amusement, but perhaps he had needed to be taken down a few pegs in his own estimation. God knew best.

When the door closed behind him, Warren glanced around the dark, cold bedchamber. A beam of pale moonlight lay across the bed. He considered lighting a lamp, looked down at Mercy, and shook his head. She would not need it. A fire in the stove, however, would dispel some of the chill and dampness. The upstairs rooms should be warmed, too, especially for that baby. But first, he would care for his wife.

Warren took one step, tripped on the rag rug, and flung his wife across the bed. She groaned again and gave a little cough, then went limp. Warren anxiously watched her face, leaning over to see if she had awakened. Her slack jaw informed him that she was oblivious to the world. A moisture-laden breeze lifted the window curtains and made him shiver. He caressed her hand; it was chilled. He needed to warm her quickly.

Gently he removed her cape, her dirty slippers, and her tattered stockings. Her new bonnet was somewhat crushed. Not knowing what else to do with it, he hung it by the ribbons from a wall hook. Rolling Mercy to her side, he unbuttoned her stained gown. It had been pretty only days earlier. Perhaps a good laundress could save it. His teeth chattered and his entire body shook with cold and agitation as he pulled the gown over his wife's head. Would she be angry when she discovered what he had done?

What else should be removed before she could sleep comfortably? Her corset. After some nervous fiddling, he discovered how to loosen its laces. The awkward contraption dropped to the floor and rocked back and forth. Next, he clumsily removed her flannel petticoats, one after another, until only pantaloons and a chemise covered her shivering form.

Mercy sighed deeply, rolled over, and snuggled into the bed, seeking warmth. Then Warren noticed her hair, still mostly in its bun. Running his fingers over her head, he pulled at anything hard and succeeded in removing all of her hairpins. They lay in a stack upon the dressing table. Her braid uncoiled down her back like a fat snake.

Warren lifted a quilt from the foot of the bed, shook it, and laid it over her. It was not enough, so he unfolded another, and another. At last she looked comfortable. He leaned over, watching her peaceful face. The hair streaming into her face bothered him; he gently pushed it over her ear with one finger. The finger strayed down her neck and along her smooth shoulder.

There came a knock at the door. Warren started guiltily and hurried to open it. "What?"

Oscar stood in the dark hallway, bearing an armful of wood and kindling. "I apologize for the intrusion, Lefty."

"This is becoming habitual," Warren remarked with some asperity.

"I wondered if you wanted a fire. This house is almighty cold. I stoked the two upstairs stoves. Naomi promised to watch Johnny's fire. She says she does not need more help tonight, but I hate to leave you alone with two women and two children to care for. If you wish, I'll sleep in the parlor and listen for Johnny."

Softening, Warren opened the door wider and followed Oscar

to the little floor stove. "I blush to admit that I had not yet considered where you would sleep, my friend. I had originally intended the spare room for you, but. . .things have changed. We could make up a pallet on the floor of that middle room upstairs."

"No, I'd best stay downstairs." Oscar quickly laid the fire and lighted it from his candle. "Tomorrow I will fix myself a place in the barn. Your uncle and his men kindly stabled the horses for us tonight. No," Oscar held up a hand, "do not apologize again. This has been a stressful day for all of us, but particularly for you. Your first responsibility during these next few days is to pamper and love your wife. She deserves a honeymoon, if any woman ever did."

"Indeed, she does. Yet I must work before play. First thing in the morning, I must shop for food; we have almost nothing in the larder."

"And I shall make myself useful by drawing bath water for everyone. Please, Lefty, do not hesitate to ask me to do anything that needs to be done. That is why I am here: to serve until you and Miss Mercy have no further need of me."

Touched, Warren bowed his head and sighed deeply. At the door, he reached out to touch the other man's arm. "Thank you. Thank you for everything. Please continue praying for me and reproving me whenever you perceive the need. I—I need that accountability. You were right: once again, I find that God is uprooting my deepest pride, and it hurts. As the Lord said to Paul on the road to Tarsus, 'It is hard for thee to kick against the pricks.' Today, I fear, I closely resembled a goaded ox. I do not wish to follow this particular path, yet it seems that I must."

Oscar gripped Warren's shoulder. "I know. I surely do know. And I also know that you will follow where He leads, and you will be thankful later that you did. Now you go back to that little woman of yours and get some rest."

"God bless you, Oscar." Warren suddenly reached out to hug his friend.

Oscar returned the quick embrace. "And you, Lefty."

After closing the door behind Oscar, Warren sat beside the stove until the fire burned to coals. Movement drew his eyes to Mercy. She sighed deeply and flung one white arm above her head. Her eyes flickered open for a moment. Warren caught his breath. She closed them again and licked her lips. Warren sighed.

After covering the coals to conserve heat, Warren at last began to undress. Moments later, he pulled the bed curtains and crept, shivering, beneath the quilts beside his wife. Longing to touch Mercy, he contented himself with taking her hand and linking his fingers through hers. He stared into the darkness until his eyelids finally drooped shut.

&

Sunlight streaming through the open window awakened Mercy. She blinked against the brightness, trying to recall her whereabouts. The room was entirely strange, although it was pleasant and cheery. White trim set off bright yellow painted walls, while the heavy mahogany furniture added a welcome contrast. The bed curtains were open, and Mercy recognized her own filthy clothing draped over a chair and a dressing table.

"Warren?" she said weakly. The only sign that he had ever been in the room was the impression of his body in the featherbed. "He was here with me. He did not leave me alone. Thank you, God." She lifted her eyes to the ceiling.

The quilts fell away when she sat up. The room was chilly, in spite of the sunlight. Mercy climbed out of bed and suddenly noticed her scanty attire. She could not recall undressing herself the night before. Pressing both hands to her cheeks, she tried to imagine Warren removing her gown. It was impossible to visualize.

Did he see my bruises? Lips pursed, she inspected the purple mark on her shoulder where Naomi had punched her. *Perhaps he overlooked it. He certainly could not have seen the welt on my thigh.* Naomi's flying foot had inflicted that injury. Mercy still felt somewhat stiff and battered from the wrestling match she had waged with the raging, agonized woman two nights before. *What would Warren say if he knew?*

There was fresh water in the pitcher on the dressing table. Beside a tin of scented soap, a fat sponge lay atop an embroidered towel. Mercy poured still-warm water into the china basin. Such luxury! How wonderful it felt to sponge her face clean! She thoroughly soaked the soft sponge, then dabbed it along her arms and around her neck. Water trickled down her chest and back, soaking her chemise, yet she did not care; it felt so good to sponge off the dirt and dried sweat.

The door opened. Mercy spun around and clutched the sponge to her chest. Its remaining water gushed into a puddle at her feet. Shocked, she could only stare at her husband. He was fully clothed, appearing as neat and clean as ever. Mercy felt like a bedraggled mud hen in his elegant presence.

Warren quickly closed the door and leaned against it. "I. . .I beg your pardon. I was unaware that you had risen. . . . I came to tell you that Oscar has drawn you a bath." As he spoke, his eyes inspected her up and down. "Did you sleep well?"

"Yes," she squeaked.

His brows suddenly lowered. He stepped toward her. Heart racing, she stared up at him. He was looking at her bruised shoulder. One hand reached out, and she felt his gentle touch. "What happened?"

"I. . .I. . .When I was helping Naomi, she struck blindly at me. I do not think she intended to harm me." It was hard to tell the truth, but a lie would have been far worse. "Are you. . . are you still angry with me, Mr. Somerville?"

To her complete confusion, he bent and kissed her bruised shoulder. She could not restrain a gasp. His hands gently gripped her upper arms. "My dear, can you forgive your husband's selfish, senseless anger? There is much that I need to learn from you about love, about caring for my neighbor, about selfless giving, about forgiveness." His hands slid down her arms, then roamed across her back. Mercy nearly collapsed upon the floor; her legs felt like jelly.

"I love you, Mercedes Somerville."

The sponge landed near the bed. She twined both arms about her husband's neck, buried her hands in his curly hair, and fervently returned his kisses. His embrace lifted her feet from the floor. Suddenly she pulled back.

Warren inspected her face through heavy-lidded eyes. "Is something wrong?"

"Granny said a preacher would not want his wife to be. . .to be carnal-minded. She said I should flee youthful lusts—"

"Granny knows nothing about this preacher, obviously. It pleases me to know that you enjoy my touch, my kisses. For a time there, I feared that you found me abhorrent. I cannot tell how much sleep I lost, wondering what I had done or said to disgust you, worrying that you simply found me unattractive."

"You, unattractive?"

Mercy's disbelieving stare made Warren smile. "Yes, me."

Thumping footsteps approached along the hallway. "Mercy? Lefty? Are you in there?"

Warren dropped his face into the curve of Mercy's neck and groaned. "Not again!"

Mercy tried to pull away, but Warren held on. "Yes, Johnny," he answered resignedly. "We are here. Wait but a few minutes, and we will come out."

With one last kiss to his wife's earlobe, he reluctantly released her. "Your bath awaits, my lady. Johnny, Oscar, and I have already bathed; we allowed you ladies some extra sleep."

"And I did fully avail myself of the opportunity," Mercy smiled. Cold and wet, she shivered in the absence of his embrace. "Where can I find this hot bath?"

"Down the hall to your left." He sounded distracted. "You do look most fetching this morning, my wife."

Blushing, Mercy grabbed her dress and hid behind it. "I must have a bath before I am fit to be seen."

He gave her a slow smile. "I hold a dissenting opinion. Later I shall explain it to you in detail. But for now, I suppose we must associate with the rest of the world. Oscar is right: we do need a honeymoon."

thirteen

Not by works of righteousness which we have done,
but according to his mercy he saved us.
Titus 3:5

"Sugar, you are hardly what I was expecting to find, although Mr. Wyeth did mention that he found you quite charming. However did Somerville discover a gem like you, hidden back in the wilderness? And how is your slave woman doing, and the baby? Nathan told me how bravely you assisted with the baby's delivery—and you such a young thing! How traumatic it must have been!"

The feather in Sophronia Wyeth's bonnet waved as she bobbed her head about. Mercy found herself watching it instead of meeting the kind lady's eyes. She had never before been addressed as "Sugar"—Mrs. Wyeth's favorite endearment. Mercy found the term particularly incongruous when applied to Warren in Sophronia's exaggerated drawl.

"You know, I was determined not to like you, since I had so wanted to match our nephew with one of our local belles, but I can see right now that any attempt to harden my heart would be futile. With a touch of my help, you will outshine them all, Mercedes, sugar. Your face is lovely despite those freckles; your hair is excellent, thick and shiny; and your figure is quite fine."

Mercy saw her husband nod hearty agreement behind his aunt's back, and her face grew hot. The jester! He would render her quite incapable of polite speech if he kept staring at her in such a fashion.

"Mr. Wyeth told me that your wedding clothes became stained during your journey. As a bridal gift, Mr. Wyeth and I wish to provide you with a modest trousseau and a wedding trip to New Bern. Since we have no children of our own, this gives us great pleasure."

Mercy glanced at Warren. All day, since their encounter in the bedchamber, he had watched her with that enigmatic smile. Every time she looked his way, she felt herself blush. "It sounds lovely, Mrs. Wyeth," she murmured.

"Concerning the trip, I will have to speak to the church board—"

Mrs. Wyeth interrupted Warren, "Oh, that is already taken care of. Mr. Wyeth spoke with the other board members and obtained their consent. I'm sure it will be discussed at the meeting tonight."

"The board meeting!" Warren groaned. "I had forgotten."

"Eight o'clock at the Drapers' home. I have arranged for all the wives to be present, sugar. It will be a sort of informal reception for your lovely Mercedes—along with that bothersome business, of course. Olivia Reynolds is in charge of refreshments, and Lila Nottingham has arranged the entertainment—all with only three days' notice! Our set is nothing if not resourceful, you will soon discover." Satisfied, Sophronia sat back with a rustle of satin and lace.

Warren and Mercy exchanged apprehensive glances.

"It sounds. . .delightful. Um, would you care for tea, Mrs. Wyeth?" Mercy meekly offered.

Sophronia rose with flapping hands. "Oh, no, thank you, sugar! I do not expect you to entertain so soon after your arrival. There will be time for such things after you have set up your household. In fact, I plan to send Bonny over today to help with your cooking until you can make more permanent arrangements. A new bride should never be bothered with such things. Mr. Wyeth tells me that your maidservant is likely to be poorly for some time yet, and you must have help with the housework. Mr. Somerville knows Bonny; she will be pleased to assist you. I imagine you will begin to receive wedding gifts soon. Ask me, and I will tell you the proper way to respond to them. Now, until this evening, my dears!"

Mercy showed her first guest to the door, timidly attempting to express her gratitude. Sophronia merely kissed her upon the forehead and patted her cheek. "Nonsense, child. Why, you are family now! See you in a few hours." After a dutiful kiss from Warren, Mrs. Wyeth took her leave.

The newlyweds stared at one another.

"I had no idea what they were planning, Mercy," Warren began. "I completely forgot about this board meeting—"

"Whatever shall I wear?" she wailed.

"That is inconsequential," he brushed her concerns aside. "You and I must come to an understanding about our position hereafter regarding the issue of slavery."

"We must?"

"Yes. I am certain this will be the major topic of discussion at the meeting tonight. Come, my dear, let us sit down." He drew her back into the sitting room and pulled her on to the settee beside him. "It is good that the topic has arisen, for, considering the events of these past few days, we need to clarify our opinions on the subject. It is one thing to espouse one's views about the hypothetical subject on paper, and another thing altogether to put one's beliefs into practice."

Mercy nodded uncertainly. "I did not purchase Naomi for personal gain," she began.

"I know. After much prayer—and a justified reprimand from Oscar—I do understand your entirely altruistic motives. My unbending adherence to principle was, in this particular, gravely inappropriate. It was arrogance speaking, Mercy—my besetting sin. Only moments before Mr. Wyeth and I reached town, I had stated unequivocally that I would never own a slave. I was unable to accept my own error. You were right; I was wrong."

At a loss for words, Mercy reached up to touch his troubled face. "What. . .what shall we do?"

"I am of the opinion that we should wait until Naomi is restored to full health, then take steps to grant her freedom—

and the baby's, too, of course. I am uncertain about the laws regarding these matters in North Carolina. We shall offer her a job as our maidservant, but she will be free to accept or refuse this offer."

"Thank you, Warren," Mercy whispered.

"And regarding our future here in Beaufort. . ." Warren sighed, looking pensive. "That rests, as always, entirely in God's hands. We must be honest about our views concerning slavery, but we must also be aware that conviction of sin is the Holy Spirit's work, not ours. These people, each one of them, need to be loved and accepted, with all their flaws and prejudices. As George Whitefield once said, 'There, but for the grace of God, go I.' Whenever I begin thinking myself uniquely virtuous, God has a way of reminding me of my sinful humanity."

"So our role here is to let God love through us."

"Exactly. And if we must suffer, let us suffer for doing what is right in God's sight. Now, I am aware that your mind will not be at rest until you decide on a dress for tonight. Don't worry about impressing these people, my dearest. You are a minister's wife, not a belle of the *beau monde*."

"The what?"

He smiled. "The fashionable set. Simply be yourself, and let God decide our future." Warren rose along with her, kissed her hand, and excused himself. "I must speak with Oscar regarding a few matters."

❧

Mercy knocked at the closed door. "Naomi? Are you awake?"

She heard a shuffling inside, and the door opened, revealing Naomi's sober face. "Miz Mercy?" Her eyes lowered and widened. "My, but you look fine."

"Thank you. This is my best gown. Do you think it is too fancy for a meeting with the church board members?" Mercy brushed her hands across the soft folds of her blue skirt. "What I wanted to ask is: do you have any experience at arranging hair? I haven't the first idea how to fix my hair to go with this dress. I can't attend the meeting with a braid hanging down my back. What a first impression that would give! I don't want to look like an unrefined miss just out of the schoolroom. I have crimping irons, but I'm so afraid that I'll char my hair instead of curling it."

Naomi's full lips twitched. Was it a smile? "I used to fix my mistress's hair."

Mercy's face lit up. "Did you? Would you, oh, please, would you help me fix my hair? I'm supposed to be ready in less than an hour."

Naomi nodded. "Just a minute."

"I hope you are feeling better. Bonny tells me you ate well at supper, for which I am thankful. Isn't Bonny a dear? Is the baby sleeping?" Mercy asked, trying to peep over Naomi's shoulder. From what she could see, the room was spotlessly clean. "Have you named her yet?"

"She ain't sleepin', but she's quiet." Naomi turned back with the infant in her arms.

"If you want to bring her down to my chamber, we could lay her on the bed. Oh, Naomi, she is so sweet!" Mercy pulled aside the baby's wrappings to admire the tiny round face.

The compliment to her daughter evidently pleased Naomi. Propping the little bundle against her shoulder, she patted the baby's back and followed Mercy downstairs into the master bedchamber.

The baby was happy to lie upon a quilt and look around with wide, curious eyes. While her child was content, Naomi began to brush out Mercy's long hair with firm, expert strokes. "You have pretty hair, Miz Mercy."

"Thank you, Naomi. I always used to wish it was golden and curly like my sister's hair, but now I like it the way it is. I think Warren admires it." From the tone of her voice, it was evident that Warren's opinion was the only one that mattered.

"You got the crimping irons heating?"

"Yes, I do. Naomi, I never did hear—have you named your baby yet?"

"You want to name her?"

"I? Name your baby?" Mercy was astonished. "Why, don't you want to name her? You are her mother."

"But she is your baby. You bought her."

The expressionless statements made Mercy turn on her seat, pulling her hair from Naomi's grasp. "No. She is your baby. I only bought you because there was no other way to help you, Naomi. Mr. Somerville and I have already discussed the matter of your freedom. As soon as you are healthy, we will have the papers drawn up. You and your baby are to be free. I would love to have you stay here and work for us, but that choice is yours. You don't have to fix my hair if you don't want to. You don't have to do anything if you don't want to."

Naomi froze. Her eyes looked dazed. "Why?" she finally croaked. "I don't deserve nothin' from you, Miz Mercy. Nothin' 'cept a beating for the way I abused you."

Tears burned Mercy's eyes. "God forgives us because He loves us, not because we deserve His grace. Jesus died for you and me on the cross, taking the punishment for our sins. He did not have to do it; He did it because He loves us so much. Mr. Somerville and I try always to treat others the way God has treated us—with grace and mercy. Because God loves you, I love you, too, Naomi." Her voice choked up when she saw tears trickling down Naomi's brown cheeks.

"Turn around or I'll never get your hair ready in time," Naomi snapped, though her hands were gentle. She worked in silence, punctuated only by assorted sniffs and snorts. Mercy found a spare handkerchief in her top drawer and offered it to the other young woman.

Their eyes met as they blew their noses in chorus. Naomi reluctantly returned Mercy's smile. "Is grace the same thing as mercy?" she suddenly asked.

"It means undeserved favor and kindness. Yes, I believe it means much the same thing as mercy. Why?"

"My baby's name is Grace. I name her after you, Miz Mercy."

"Oh, Naomi! I am honored." Mercy's nose began to run again as her eyes filled with tears.

"If you don't stop that cryin', your eyes will be all red and puffy for the meetin'," Naomi warned, turning her forcefully back toward the table.

Mercy chuckled. "You are right. I will stop."

❧

"Charmed to meet you, my dear," Lila Nottingham drawled, touching her scented cheek to Mercy's. "Such a pretty thing you are."

"Thank you, ma'am."

"But then, our minister is ever so dashing and refined. 'Tis only right that he should find a charmin' companion. I hope you enjoy Beaufort. Things are quiet now, what with the holidays approachin', but they will liven up come spring."

"I am pleased to be here. I find your town quite. . .charming." It seemed to be the adjective of the evening, and Mercy was too tired to think of another.

"I hope you'll come visit us soon. My husband has only just returned from a sea voyage. He wishes to become acquainted with Mr. Somerville and you, sugar."

There was that "sugar" word again. "I'm sure we will be pleased to visit you and your husband, Mrs. Nottingham. Thank you for your kind welcome." Mercy knew she had a Southern drawl of her own, but her accent was slight when compared to the affected speech of these Beaufort ladies.

Meanwhile, the men greeted Captain Nottingham cheerfully and introduced him to Warren. Mercy had little opportunity to study the whiskery gentleman sailor, for the ladies claimed her attention. The group of men appeared amicable and cheerful. Perhaps Warren had been mistaken and there would be no confrontation this evening.

Olivia Reynolds seemed to be a kindly little woman, though she seldom had a chance to speak. Mrs. Dabney Carson, Mrs. Orville Draper, and Mrs. Horace Moore pelted Mercy with questions about her family and background, all the while nibbling their tiny cakes and cookies. Mrs. Wyeth thoroughly enjoyed introducing her new niece to her "set."

"So this is the bride of our lucky young parson."

Mercy looked up into a kindly, bearded face and smiled.

"Oh, Dion, I forgot that you hadn't yet been introduced. Mrs. Somerville, dear, this is Dionysius West, the town's favorite bachelor. Doctor, meet our lovely Mrs. Mercedes Somerville," Sophronia cheerfully introduced them.

Mercy offered her hand and was startled when the gentleman bowed and kissed it. "Welcome, my dear. You are a pleasant sight for these old eyes."

"Old, indeed!" Mrs. Wyeth chuckled. "You've not yet attained thirty years, Dion. Now leave this young thing to us ladies before her husband takes exception to your flirtation." She shooed him away with her fan.

Just then a burly gentleman rose to his feet and noisily cleared his throat. Leaning heavily on a cane, Mr. Reynolds scanned the crowded parlor from beneath his bushy brows. "It is time we discussed our business." After draining the last drops from his glass, he beckoned a servant closer and indicated his need of a refill. The other men turned in their seats to face Reynolds, and general conversation ceased except for a few hushed whispers between Mrs. Carson and Mrs. Moore.

"The other night we agreed to suspend judgment on an important matter until Mr. Wyeth and Mr. Somerville had opportunity for discussion and compromise. Since that time it has come to my attention that Mr. Somerville has wisely altered his stance and purchased for himself a servant."

The subsequent murmur of approval widened Mercy's eyes. She looked at Warren and thought some of the healthy color drained from his face.

"Therefore I wish to repeat my offer of the other night with a minor alteration: instead of hiring out a servant to you, Somerville, I plan to gift you and your wife with a trained page and a cook." His naturally ruddy face shone with self-satisfaction.

There were gasps of surprise and admiration. Mercy overheard Mrs. Nottingham whisper to Mrs. Moore, "My, how generous! I wonder what Olivia thinks about the old blowhard giving away her trained servants."

Warren slowly rose to his feet. Mercy hoped his leg would support him; it seemed to give way at the worst possible times. He approached Mr. Reynolds and extended his hand. Reynolds took it in a hearty grip, studying the younger man's face with narrowed eyes.

"I am sure I can speak for my wife when I say that we are overwhelmed by the benevolence you have bestowed upon us," Warren addressed the gathering. "You have gone out of your way to make us feel welcome. Such thoughtfulness cannot but be pleasing to our Lord, who often instructed his people to let their hospitality be known to all."

Warren beckoned toward Mercy. Responding to the message in his eyes, she almost jumped to her feet and hurried forward. He reached for her hand and held it tightly.

He took a deep breath. "Concerning your generous gift, Mr. Reynolds"—the intervening silence was oppressive—"We gratefully accept."

A collective sigh of relief rose from the audience.

"However," Mercy felt her husband's grip on her hand tighten. "I cannot deceive you by pretending to embrace the practice of slavery as just and moral. My wife and I hold strong objections to the slave trade, and we believe that God created all men equal—men of every skin color, every race, every creed."

Mr. Reynolds tried to interrupt, but Warren held up a restraining hand. "Hear me out, sir. In the event we accept the gift of these servants, we will subsequently grant them their freedom, as we plan to grant freedom to our maidservant Naomi. Should they wish to work for us, we will gladly employ them and keep them in our home, treating them as our equals in the eyes of God. Our equals, I say, for are we not all, in a sense, servants? As Jesus said in Matthew, chapter twenty: 'Whosoever will be chief among you, let him be your servant.' Christ freely demonstrated love to all people: merchant or prostitute, influential or outcast, rich or poor. As His followers, how can we do less?"

Mercy felt Warren shaking, though his voice was clear and steady. She squeezed his hand and moved closer to indicate her support and agreement.

"I must make one thing clear to you: although my wife and I hold our convictions firmly and dearly, we will not force our beliefs upon anyone. We were called by God to minister to His saints and to spread the gospel to every living creature. In so doing, I will not hesitate to assert my convictions; I will preach as the Holy Spirit leads; I will not turn a blind eye to evil in the midst of the flock. Nevertheless, I promise also that I will not attempt to forcibly overhaul your traditions, values, or consciences—that is neither my place nor my intention.

"Now, my friends and brothers, you are fully apprised of our standing, and I trust that you will decide the matter of my continued employment prayerfully and prudently. Mrs. Somerville and I will withdraw from your midst, leaving you free to discuss the matter at your leisure. Thank you."

With a polite bow, Warren drew Mercy after him toward the door, where a servant handed over their wraps. Instead of requesting the Wyeths' carriage to take them home, Warren started off down the street. "We can walk. It is but a short distance."

Mercy attempted to match her husband's rapid, uneven strides. "Are you sure walking is a good idea, Warren? Your leg—"

"I can manage," he snapped.

Subdued, Mercy walked silently beside him.

When they reached the house, Oscar quietly informed them: "Naomi is upstairs—haven't seen her since supper. Bonny cleaned up the kitchen and went home; said she'd be back early to fix breakfast."

"How was Johnny?" Mercy asked while hanging up her cloak.

"That young rascal is lying awake up there yet. Insists he can't go to sleep until you each give him a hug and listen to his prayers."

Without a word, Warren headed upstairs to Johnny's room. Mercy paused on the bottom step to say, "Oscar, thank you for watching Johnny for us tonight."

"Is something amiss?" Oscar asked in concern. "Lefty looks troubled."

Mercy chewed her lower lip. "The meeting. It was difficult." In a few words, she explained about Reynolds' offer and Warren's response.

Oscar shook his head. "But he spoke calmly? With respect and restraint?"

"It was almost like seeing Jesus before his accusers—Warren spoke with such love and humility! We prayed together before we left this evening. You see, he expected something like this to happen tonight."

"The Lord prepared his heart," Oscar agreed. "I was praying, and I'll keep on praying, Miz Mercy. I believe God has a future for you two in this here town of Beaufort. If He wants you here, no number of board members can override His vote."

Mercy met Oscar's honest gaze and could not help returning his gentle smile. "You are so very right! Oh, Oscar, what would we do without you?" She stood on tiptoe and kissed his cheek before hurrying upstairs after her husband.

❧

Mercy was still awake when Warren climbed into bed. Long into the night he had paced the sitting-room floor, reading his Bible and praying. To Mercy's great disappointment, he had wanted to be alone. Her pillow was damp with tears.

She rolled toward him. His broad back faced her. Pushing aside feelings of rejection, she shyly reached out to rub his taut shoulders and neck.

He jumped, startled. "Did I wake you?"

"No, I could not sleep." She put both hands to work, squeezing his shoulders and arms, massaging along his spine, enjoying the feel of his muscles through his nightshirt. She found the distinct dent in his shoulder blade, just as her brothers had described, and made a wry face. *Thank You for keeping him alive all those years ago, Lord.* When Warren remained silent, she rubbed his temples and forehead. His nightcap slipped off, and his curls tickled her palms.

At last he heaved a tremulous sigh. "Mercy, I am so very sorry."

"For what, dear?"

Emotion choked his voice. "For bringing you here into this. . .terrible uncertainty. I had no idea—I never dreamed this issue would descend upon us so quickly. Now I believe it probable that we will be asked to leave. It would not trouble me had I only myself to support, but what about you and Johnny? What of Naomi, Oscar, and the baby?"

"Grace. The baby's name is Grace," she informed him. "Dearest Warren, do not worry yourself so. God will provide for us. If it is not His will for us to remain in Beaufort, He will show us His plan in good time."

"Had I not recklessly insisted upon marrying you at once, I would have known about this before the vows were taken."

"And then what? Would you have left me at the altar? I cannot agree that it would have been better thus." Pushing up on one hand, she leaned over his shoulder. "Warren, all your fretting will not change what is. As for me, I am so very thankful that we have each other. Had I a choice, I would be nowhere in the world except here with you."

All at once he rolled over and wrapped both arms around her. His face pressed into her chest, and his body shuddered.

Lying back against the headboard, Mercy cradled her husband in her arms, stroked his back, smoothed his wild hair, and tried to calm her racing heart. "Do not chasten yourself for mistakes of the past, my dear. God promises to work these things together for good in our lives. My faith in you is unshaken, Warren. I told Oscar earlier that when you spoke before those people tonight, you reminded me of

Jesus standing before His accusers. I believe you behaved exactly as God would have wanted. I am so very proud to be the wife of Warren Somerville! I love you dearly, my husband."

She pressed a tender kiss upon his head. He turned his face to the side and snuggled even closer. "I have longed to hear you say that you love me. Oh, Mercy, I love you so!"

"I have always loved you, Warren. You should know that." She caressed his face with trembling fingers, wiping away his hot tears.

"Tell me often, Mercy. Never take for granted that I know your thoughts and feelings."

"You are right. It seems that we both assumed too much and trusted too little. I was afraid, but no longer."

For a minute more they lay quietly. Mercy felt his warmth, his breath, the beat of his heart. She knew exactly when he ceased to think of his troubles and became acutely aware of his wife.

"At this hour, I do not believe we will hear a knock at the door," she murmured amid his fervent kiss.

fourteen

"Not by might, nor by power, but by my spirit,"
saith the Lord of hosts.
Zechariah 4:6

"Our time here may be of short duration, but we will enjoy it to the utmost," Warren told his wife the next afternoon as they strolled slowly along the oceanfront.

"It is delightful, Warren. The people here are so warm and friendly! I cannot but believe that they think very highly of you. At each home we have called upon today, I have heard only unstinting praise for your sermons."

"It is most gratifying. But, of course, the message is the Lord's, not mine. I wonder when you will first hear me speak? I have tried to picture your face in the congregation." Warren squeezed his elbow close, hugging her hand against his side. "Are you warm enough, my dear? This ocean breeze holds a sharp bite."

Mercy lifted her face to meet the pale winter sunshine. Gulls mewed along the seashore, and the constant hushing roll of distant ocean waves enchanted her ears. "I enjoy the lovely fresh air, Warren. Do not trouble yourself about me." Although his face glowed with love and contentment, she had heard the undertone of sadness in his expressive voice.

"We will have many years together, Lord willing, and I will witness countless sermons." She smiled up at him and squeezed his arm against her body.

He gave her a glance from the corners of his eyes. "Seeking to command my attention again, are you? It is indeed an effective ploy."

She hurriedly backed away, blushing to her ears. "Do not

remind me of that day! I was so humiliated. I thought I had disgusted you entirely."

He caught her by the arm before she could move out of reach and tucked her hand back under his elbow. "Not at all. Your naive behavior was quite flattering and, uh, eye-opening. However, I would not recommend that you try it on any other man."

"Why not?" She gave him a fluttering glance.

He looked pointedly around at their surroundings. "I think it best that we suspend this discourse until our situation is private. You are provoking me every moment to kiss you or throttle you—one or the other—and public murder is frowned upon in these parts." He helped her to the boardwalk lining the street.

"Very well; I will be good. What is our next call?"

"Mrs. Munfrees and her son, Jonathan. I believe you will approve of them. She is a sea widow. Jonathan admires my horse first, my sermons second. I had thought that perhaps he and Johnny could become acquainted."

"That would be nice. Although Johnny adores you and Oscar, he needs playmates nearer his age."

"I enjoy Johnny's society, but at present you are my companion of choice."

"So I am to be supplanted someday in your affections?" she inquired in mock consternation.

Unwilling to exchange another repartee, he stopped to look into her eyes. "Never. I wish only that our companionship should continue forever. Would that I could keep you entirely to myself, if only for a day. Sometime soon I plan to row you out to the barrier islands. We can walk there alone upon the sand, and no one will disturb us," Warren warmed to his topic. "In summer we can go sea bathing in a private cove—"

A voice called from behind them. "Mr. Somerville, wait, please!"

Warren stopped and turned, swinging Mercy gently around with him. A high-stepping pony drawing a light cart made a rapid approach. The driver waved urgently.

"Dabney Carson." Warren's voice held surprise and some reserve.

Mercy glanced at her husband, then back to the other gentleman whose round, red face shone with eagerness. He had been at the board meeting, she recalled. Carson quickly tied his pony's reins and hopped to the ground, reaching for Warren's hand.

"Good day, Mrs. Somerville." Recalling his manners, he gave Mercy a perfunctory nod. Without waiting for a reply, he turned back to Warren. "Reverend Somerville, you are, in fact, the owner of the remarkable carriage that is parked behind the carriage works? The black one with yellow trim and the fantastic carvings on its doors?"

"I am."

"And might you be willing to sell? I am a serious collector of fine vehicles, you see, and this one is a find, an amazing find of a peculiarity I never expected to discover in my lifetime. In my youth, I once saw President Washington himself driven to a society event in such a carriage—I had believed his coach to be unique, but I now know I was mistaken. It must be the work of a master carriage maker, a hand-crafted work of art!"

Mercy felt Warren's muscles tighten beneath her hand. He said only, "I believe we could come to a reasonable agreement, sir."

"May I stop by the parsonage this evening? I shall have my lawyer draw up the appropriate papers, and I shall speak to my banker. You will find my offer to be generous, I am certain."

Warren nodded soberly. "It will be a pleasure to do business with you, sir. You do understand that the vehicle is in need of repair?"

"But that is my specialty! Restoring such a prize will provide me with delight beyond measure." Mr. Carson pumped Warren's hand. At last he genuinely acknowledged Mercy. "You look lovely today, Mrs. Somerville. My wife extends her greetings."

"Thank you, sir. I enjoyed making her acquaintance last evening."

"You must be proud of this fine young man, your husband. Beaufort has never before heard so eloquent an advocate of the Holy Scriptures. We are blessed to have such a clergyman here."

"I am indeed proud, sir."

Warren was speechless.

Carson nodded affably for a moment, paused with knitted brows, then inquired hesitantly, "You have spoken to West? He was to drop by the parsonage today and report the board's decision."

Warren could only shake his head.

"We voted to keep you on, son. I'll admit that I voted nay, but now I'm glad to have been voted down. The Lord knows best about these things. West is right: you're the finest preacher ever seen or heard in these parts. If we can't overlook a few minor differences of opinion, the church isn't long for this world. Love put in practice, and so on. That reminds me, we also approved Wyeth's suggestion of a short holiday for the two of you—maybe next week? Got to start a young couple off right! West says he'll fill the pulpit for a Sunday. That should prove entertaining. Well, good afternoon to you both." He doffed his top hat, climbed back into the cart, and drove away.

The couple again walked in thoughtful silence. Mercy glanced up at Warren and caught him grinning. She began to chuckle, and he suddenly laughed aloud. With a suddenness that took her breath away, he grasped her by the waist, lifted her into the air, and spun around.

"Warren, really!" she protested when he landed her back on her feet. "Be careful of your leg! What will people think?" Reaching up, she secured her bonnet more firmly.

"What people? Look around you; there is no one to observe us." He laughed again.

"Nonsensical man. What are you thinking?"

"Oh, Mercy mine, I am wild with astonishment! I am thinking, 'Oh, ye of little faith!' This is truly an incredible turn of events. It is entirely the Lord's doing." He chuckled again, "And what would your father say? He told me repeatedly that the coach was valuable, and did I believe him? Decidedly, no!"

"Now we should be able to purchase a nice new carriage. And now I can freely admit that I adore our house here, Warren. It would have been so very hard to leave it! We simply must hurry home to tell Oscar, Bonny, Naomi, and Johnny!"

"Lord, Your ways are inscrutable," Warren mused softly, still grinning. "Thank You for Your amazing and bountiful mercy, Lord. For that matter, thank You for *my* Mercy."

౿

Mrs. Somerville thoroughly enjoyed her first Sunday in Beaufort. After accompanying Warren on many social calls that week, she recognized enough faces to keep from feeling overwhelmed. The singing was exceptional, especially that of the slaves in the loft. From her front row seat, Mercy peeked over her shoulder and saw Oscar's smiling face above her. His rich bass voice could not be mistaken. Without a second thought, she smiled back.

Warren's clear tenor was also pleasant to her ear. Angel duet, Calvin had described his two friends' singing. Mercy determined there and then that she would demand a private performance from Oscar and Warren at her earliest opportunity.

Johnny squirmed beside her on the seat. He had already met several new playmates in town, finding a special friend in Jonathan Munfrees. Seeing her small brother make signs to the older boy across the aisle, Mercy laid a hand on his knee and shook her head. Johnny looked at her, looked up front at Warren, and sat back in his seat with a sigh.

Warren looked so tall and handsome, standing at the lectern. She had never before seen him wearing vestments. The black robe and white collar complimented his aristocratic face. No wonder all the church ladies swooned over their new minister.

Mercy smiled at the thought, feeling entirely contented. He was her man from the top of his curly head to the soles of his feet. His ardent devotion had laid her every fear to rest.

Dear Lord, I hardly know how to thank You! Please continue to banish my doubts and build my confidence in Your provision for me and for my family. I know that You will care for my loved ones back in Woods Grove. Please help me to concentrate on doing what I can to help others, and keep me from worrying about things I cannot do. As Warren often says, I must trust in You and obey. Thank you for Warren. You knew exactly what sort of man I needed to marry.

She lifted her head as Warren began to speak.

"I ask you to open your Bibles today to the Gospel of Matthew, chapter three. In previous weeks we have studied the story of the nativity. We shall now continue our survey of the life of Jesus Christ, the life that is our perfect example of godly living. How much each one of us must learn about being lights in this dark world! With our countless faults, our blind spots, and our sinful natures, we are imperfect tools at best, yet God makes use of us in forwarding His perfect plans. . . ."

Mercy opened her Bible to the correct passage, and settled back to listen and learn.

A Letter To Our Readers

Dear Reader:

In order that we might better contribute to your reading enjoyment, we would appreciate your taking a few minutes to respond to the following questions. We welcome your comments and read each form and letter we receive. When completed, please return to the following:

Rebecca Germany, Fiction Editor
Heartsong Presents
PO Box 719
Uhrichsville, Ohio 44683

1. Did you enjoy reading *Grant Me Mercy?*
   ❑ Very much. I would like to see more books
      by this author!
   ❑ Moderately
      I would have enjoyed it more if _____

      _____

      _____

2. Are you a member of **Heartsong Presents**? Yes ❑ No ❑
   If no, where did you purchase this book? _____

   _____

3. How would you rate, on a scale from 1 (poor) to 5 (superior),
   the cover design? _____

4. On a scale from 1 (poor) to 10 (superior), please rate the
   following elements.

   _____ Heroine   _____ Plot

   _____ Hero   _____ Inspirational theme

   _____ Setting   _____ Secondary characters

5. These characters were special because_____

_____

_____

6. How has this book inspired your life?_____

_____

_____

7. What settings would you like to see covered in future
   Heartsong Presents books?_____

_____

_____

8. What are some inspirational themes you would like to see
   treated in future books?_____

_____

_____

9. Would you be interested in reading other **Heartsong
   Presents** titles?   Yes ❏   No ❏

10. Please check your age range:
    ❏ Under 18   ❏ 18-24   ❏ 25-34
    ❏ 35-45   ❏ 46-55   ❏ Over 55

11. How many hours per week do you read?_____

Name _____

Occupation _____

Address _____

City _____ State _____ Zip _____